"WE CAN'T IGNORE WHAT'S HAPPENED, JILL."

He leaned over the bed and caught her hand. "There was something electric between us. You can't deny it."

"Oh, Greg," she whispered. "We've already broken the rule we agreed on. We can't afford to jeopardize our working relationship for a brief love affair."

"Then wouldn't we be better off staying as lovers? We always get along." Grimacing at her dry expression, he clarified. "Okay, we *usually* get along. The problems in the past few days are because our auras have been clashing and our stars have just been circling in the wrong orbits."

"Are you sure you're not saying this just to get me into bed again and have your way with me?" she asked, smiling.

Greg looked at her longingly. "I wouldn't have far to go right now . . ."

CANDLELIGHT ECSTASY ROMANCES®

WRITTEN IN THE STARS

Linda Randall Wisdom

A CANDLELIGHT ECSTASY ROMANCE®

Published by
Dell Publishing Co., Inc.
1 Dag Hammarskjold Plaza
New York, New York 10017

ISBN: 0-440-19798-8

Printed in the United States of America

First printing—January 1986

To Our Readers:

We have been delighted with your enthusiastic response to Candlelight Ecstasy Romances®, and we thank you for the interest you have shown in this exciting series.

In the upcoming months we will continue to present the distinctive, sensuous love stories you have come to expect only from Ecstasy. We look forward to bringing you many more books from your favorite authors and also the very finest work from new authors of contemporary romantic fiction.

As always, we are striving to present the unique, absorbing love stories that you enjoy most—books that are more than ordinary romance. Your suggestions and comments are always welcome. Please write to us at the address below.

Sincerely,

The Editors
Candlelight Romances
1 Dag Hammarskjold Plaza
New York, New York 10017

CHAPTER ONE

The airline terminal of an international airport shouldn't be deserted and quiet, unless it is two o'clock in the morning and the last flight has just limped in well over an hour late. The returning passengers found the halls not as well lit as usual and the cleaning crews busy vacuuming carpets and emptying ashtrays for the coming day.

The disembarking passengers resembled zombies with their glazed eyes and weary-looking bodies as they walked to the escalator leading to the baggage carousel. One woman, holding a soft leather carry-on and with a garment bag hanging over her shoulder, swept past the passengers milling about and left through the pneumatic doors with the ease of an experienced traveler. Even at that late hour a few of the men admired the classic beauty of her features and the slim body evident under the tan down coat, which flapped open to reveal a silk sweater the color of rich paprika and designer jeans. Her low, cuffed suede boots were meant more for comfort than style, and her tawny blond shoulder-length hair was swept back in a fishtail braid secured with a band of soft velvet. It was apparent that she wasn't expecting to be met by anyone but determined to reach the final destination of her trip.

The security guard at the door lifted a hand in greeting to the woman. "See you finally made it," he commented with the familiarity of someone who knew a regular traveler.

She nodded, smiling wryly. "Never suffer through a layover in Chicago, Frank, if you want to arrive home at a decent hour," she replied, switching her bag to her other hand and looking around for a taxi. Luckily there were still a few hardy cabbies waiting in the hope of securing a fare into the city.

"Hey, you feeling okay Ms. Blake?" the guard asked with concern, not missing her abnormally pale features.

"Too much traveling in too short a time," she explained, stepping forward to one of the waiting cabs.

"Take it easy," the guard called after her.

Jill sank down onto the backseat and gave her address to the driver. She leaned her head back and closed her eyes, hoping her queasy stomach would soon settle. At the moment she wasn't sure if it was due to the bumpy flight, the lemon sole she had eaten for dinner, or the beginning stages of the flu. Due to her hectic schedule the past month, she wouldn't be surprised if her resistance was down. All she cared about now was getting home so she could take some aspirin, drink a large glass of orange juice and crawl into her comfortable bed. She only hoped her topsy-turvy stomach would hold off engaging in any energetic acrobatics until she reached the safety of her home.

Jill couldn't remember when she had ever felt so tired from a three-day trip. She grimaced at the knowledge that Greg would give her a lecture about her stubborn nature when he saw her in the morning. He had insisted that he should be the one to travel to Boston this time, but she had dug in her heels. After all, he had made the last two trips, so it was natural for her to take her turn. Of course, he hadn't just returned from a skiing trip in Aspen or had a stomach virus six weeks before. As a result, her constantly weary state surfaced during a trip she hadn't truly been physically prepared to make. Now she felt tired and out of sorts. She pulled a pack of cigarettes and her lighter out of her purse, but when her stomach did another flip, decided not to chance it and put them away.

A little over an hour later the taxi driver let Jill out in front of a large Victorian house situated close to Russian Hill, an area in San Francisco known for its old money and equally old names living in the large homes.

Jill smothered a yawn as she unlocked the heavy door that boasted an old-fashioned stained glass window and entered the chilly house. She silently cursed the high staircase as she slowly climbed the carpeted treads to her apartment.

Inside, her apartment was a step into another century, compared with the 1800s look of the exterior of the two-story house. Jill's living room was decorated with modern, pale wood furniture to complement the pale rose, ecru and turquoise color scheme, colors meant to soothe her after a harried day at the computer. She quickly passed through the living room to reach her bedroom, dropping her bags inside the doorway; all she cared about was undressing and pulling on a soft flannel nightgown for comforting warmth. Her body was rapidly warning her that she was best off huddled under the covers as soon as possible if she knew what was good for her. She cleaned her heated face with a damp washcloth and walked to the kitchen to pour herself a glass of ice water.

Jill hadn't taken more than two sips of water when her stomach revolted with alarming speed. With barely seconds to spare, she made it to the bathroom and almost collapsed on the tile floor. She groaned and lost track of time as the nausea overtook her again.

Time passed slowly as she lay stretched out on the floor, praying the tile would cool her heated flesh. She couldn't remember ever feeling as sick as she now did. Her stomach cramped, and it felt as if her insides were trying to climb outside her body.

It seemed like hours before she could drag herself back into the bedroom. The fire radiating from her abdomen was a warning that her illness was more than a simple case of the flu. She reached up to the telephone and punched out seven numbers. The line rang twelve times before it was picked up with a man's mumbled, " 'Lo?"

"Greg," she sobbed, holding onto the phone as if it was a lifeline. "Please, come. Something's really wrong." The clatter of the phone on the other end, plus a woman's murmured curse, was the only reply.

Jill curled up in the fetal position, trying to ease the pain in her stomach. It wasn't long before she heard sounds of heavy footsteps running up the stairs. She closed her eyes to hide the blur of the room swimming around her.

"Hi, lady." A cool hand on her forehead brought her back to the present.

Jill opened her eyes and looked up at the man, whose rugged features were etched with worry. His black hair stuck up every which way, a mute testimony to his just having gotten out of bed, and his gray eyes were shadowed with concern.

"You don't have to look as if I'm going to die on you in the next five minutes." The pain that speared her stomach just then made her cry out loud and claw at Greg's arm for support.

He didn't waste any time asking questions. His first call was to Jill's doctor and the second to an ambulance service. He picked Jill up off the floor as carefully as possible and deposited her on the bed.

"How long have you been like this?" he asked her, sitting on the edge of the bed. He pushed a stray lock of damp hair away from her face, not liking the heat coming off her skin.

"Too long. I guess Rita isn't too happy that I interrupted her beauty sleep," she croaked.

"She'll survive." There was a grim cast to his face as he listened to her cries of pain. "Do you want me to call Cal?" Greg asked quietly.

Jill shook her head. "We broke up two weeks ago," she explained, not caring to remember the scene that had precipitated the split with the man she had been seeing for the past few months. She sighed deeply. "I'm going to have to go to the hospital, aren't I?" She gripped his hand tightly as another spasm of pain swept over her.

Greg nodded. "I'm afraid so."

She moaned. "I hate hospitals! They'll poke and prod and only make me feel worse!"

He didn't want to tell her that he feared the doctor would do a great deal more than poke and prod before he finished with Jill.

"Greg." A dark-haired woman stood in the bedroom doorway. "What's going on?" Her frosty gaze swept over Jill as if she was convinced her illness was merely an illusion meant to spoil her sleep.

13

"Hello, Rita," she managed a weak greeting.

"Jill's very sick, love," Greg explained, not taking his eyes off Jill's flushed face. "I called her doctor, and an ambulance should be here any minute. Why don't you just go on back to bed?"

Jill was in pain, but she wasn't sick enough not to wonder how the voluptuous Latin woman could look so sexy at four A.M. with her blue-black hair tousled about her shoulders and a lipstick red silk kimono covering her nude body. She would have voiced her impertinent question aloud, but a splitting pain in her abdomen grabbed her attention with full force.

By the time the ambulance arrived Jill was past caring about Greg's current lover's beauty secrets. She wasn't even aware of Greg shouting orders to a sullen Rita as he followed the attendants downstairs and outside while pulling on a crewneck sweater.

The next few hours were a pain-filled haze to Jill as she was indeed poked and prodded. The diagnosis of a hot appendix wasn't what Jill wanted to hear, but she was alert enough to sign the authorization for surgery. She caught a glimpse of Greg's drawn features before the prick of a needle brought her oblivion.

Greg paced the length of the surgical waiting area, his arms crossed in front of him. His thick Irish knit sweater could have been thin cotton, judging from the chilled look about him. Rita, now dressed in red silk trousers and tunic, sat in a nearby chair, smoking a cigarette.

"I realize she's your partner, Greg, but couldn't you just have the hospital call you when she's out of surgery so we can return to the house?" she asked, crossing one shapely leg over the other. "After all, she isn't a relative, so I don't know why you're so upset over this. It was bad enough that she woke us just after we had gotten to sleep." Her dark eyes grew slumbrous as she recalled the reason for their late night.

"She's someone I care about a great deal," Greg informed her coldly.

Rita snapped to attention and ground out her cigarette in the ashtray. "I should have realized the situation much sooner." Frosty insolence replaced her sensual beauty. "Oh, I've had my suspicions during the past few months, but I knew whose bed you could be found in, so I wasn't all that worried."

Greg shook his head, unable to decipher the meaning of her words. "What are you talking about?"

She raised a hand to his cheek. "You're a wonderful lover, Greg," she said softly, with regret in her voice. "You're a man any woman would want, but I don't believe in acting as a substitute. Call me when and if you ever come to your senses." She left him after a soul-searching kiss.

Greg felt a twinge of regret as he watched Rita leave, but there was no empty feeling in his heart or sorrow over her defection; only curiosity regarding her cryptic words. A few moments later his attention was diverted by the appearance of a man wearing sweat-stained surgical scrubs.

"She's doing fine," Dr. Simmons said immediately, easing Greg's concern quickly. "I got it out before it burst, but it was a close call. I'm sure she'll be running a low temperature for the next couple of days. Naturally we'll have to keep a close eye on her to make sure she doesn't run around for several weeks."

Greg's smile warmed his stormy gray eyes. "I'll

believe it when I see it. No one has the energy level she does," he said with faint good humor. "May I see her?"

"She's in post op right now, and you can go in as long as you realize she'll be very groggy the rest of the day," the doctor explained. He viewed Greg's dark hair with amusement. "If anyone questions your right to be there, I'd advise you to tell the nurse you're her husband and not her brother. Family resemblance is extremely minimal in your case."

Greg grinned. "Maybe I should ask for a note from my doctor," he said.

"Talk about being your doctor, it's about time for your annual physical," the man recalled. "Call Diane and make an appointment."

Greg nodded, knowing this wasn't a suggestion from the crusty middle-aged man but an order. "Business must be bad if you have to solicit in the hospital," he joked, walking with Simmons to the recovery room door.

Once inside, Greg discovered that the recovery room was more intimidating than the movies portrayed. Jill looked tiny and defenseless among the white sheets, IVs and catheters. A nurse wearing scrubs was just removing a plastic cap from Jill's head and checking her vital signs. She smiled at Greg, the woman in her unable to resist his masculine appeal.

"She's coming around again," she said quietly.

Jill's eyelids lifted slowly, as if with great effort. When they finally opened all the way, she looked glassy-eyed at her visitor.

"Hi." Her voice sounded rusty.

"Hi, yourself." Relief loosened the tension in his shoulder muscles as he realized she was going to be

16

all right. Alarm tensed them again when Jill's lids drifted closed. He looked at the nurse in alarm.

"It will be awhile before she's fully awake and aware of her surroundings," she assured him. "She'll be moved upstairs to her room soon, if you'd rather wait there."

Greg took some time to call Jill's mother and his and Jill's agent before going upstairs to her room, where he found she had already been moved in the interim.

As he sat near her bed, he was gratified to see that she didn't look as pale as before and that her sleep was deep but natural.

During the next few hours Jill roused periodically, long enough to peer myopically at Greg or at the nurse as she asked Jill if she needed a pain shot or checked her IV.

Late that afternoon the doctor ordered Greg home to take some much-needed rest. He refused to pry himself from the hospital room until he received the promise that he would be contacted if there were any changes in Jill's condition.

As he rode home in the back of a taxi, the picture of Jill looking so vulnerable in the hospital bed haunted his mind, even when he later collapsed onto his rumpled bed that still bore the opulent scent of Rita's perfume.

Jill's memory of the twenty-four hours after her surgery was a vague recollection of a nurse coming in to check her IV, replace the empty one with a full bottle and give her a shot for the pain when necessary. Her mumbled words made no sense, although the nurse seemed to understand her slurred conversation.

Jill didn't return to the real world until the next

morning. When she opened her eyes, her first sight was Greg slouched in the chair near her bed. Her smile looked a trifle lopsided.

"I always hated that shirt," she rasped.

Greg looked down at his shirt, a muted plum and pale green plaid. "What's wrong with it?" he asked defensively, not revealing the great relief he experienced when he heard her speak.

"It reminds me of a hawker standing in front of a strip joint." Her eyes widened when she noticed the floral arrangements brightening the room.

"And here you always thought no one liked you," he said. "Maybe I should have my appendix out."

Jill couldn't hold back a yawn. "You had yours out when you were in high school. They don't grow back. You're just out of luck, pal."

"Want some water?"

Jill nodded, already having discovered she had trouble moving the arm that had the IV taped to it. As for her body, she was prepared to move around as little as possible.

Greg filled the small plastic cup with ice water and held it to her lips. She drank thirstily before speaking again.

"Give my apologies to Rita for upsetting your evening." She lay back against her pillow, hoping Greg wouldn't see that she really didn't mean her apology. From the first time she had met Rita, the two women had made no attempt to ease the hostility they shared. The funny thing was, Jill wasn't even entirely sure why she didn't like Rita. The woman was certainly lovely, not conceited, and she seemed to think a lot of Greg, but Jill just couldn't find it in her to like her.

"She survived," he said carelessly.

Jill's brain may have been muddled, but there was no mistaking Greg's use of the past tense.

"She dumped you, huh?" She found it difficult to feel too sorry for him. She had never felt that the steamy woman was right for Greg. She thought privately that a softer, more understanding woman was the type this warm-hearted man needed.

"Thanks for the sympathy, Jill," Greg said dryly, sitting back as the nurse came in and bestowed a warm smile on him.

"Would you mind stepping outside for a few moments, Mr. Richmond?" she asked. "I have to examine Ms. Blake."

He nodded and rose to his feet. "I'll go down to the waiting area," he said, leaving with a smile at both women.

The nurse couldn't help watching Greg walk out, and she turned back to Jill with a slightly embarrassed smile before proceeding to change her bandage, then remove her IV and catheter, much to Jill's pleasure.

"I'll let Mr. Richmond know he can come back in," the nurse said with just a faint degree of eagerness.

Jill laughed as she collapsed back against her pillow. She was beginning to think it was a shame they had never had a chance to see if they could make it as a couple. One reason they had always kept their relationship platonic was the idea that a love affair could screw up a perfectly good business partnership. Then, too, in the five years they had worked together, Jill and Greg had never seemed to be free at the same time.

Greg returned to the room ten minutes later with a faint smile on his lips.

"Lecher," Jill accused mildly, watching him sit down.

He looked at her with the proper degree of innocence. "Me?"

"You," she pronounced. "You never look at me the way you looked at the nurse."

"And I won't look at you that way as long as you wear those baggy sweatpants you usually have on when we're working," he countered. "Oh, yes, this came by special messenger." He pulled a package out of his jacket pocket and handed it to Jill.

"I think you'd better unwrap it for me." She flexed her hand, which still felt a little stiff from the IV needle.

Greg opened the box and pulled out a small furry gorilla wearing horn-rimmed glasses.

"Give me a break!" she said with a groan, closing her eyes. "That is the fifty-third Hairy Harry I've been given."

"Don't denigrate the gorilla who pays your charge accounts," he teased, setting the toy on the table.

Jill winced when she shifted her position. Greg was quick to see her reaction.

"Do you need a pain pill?" he asked quickly. "Do you want me to ask the nurse if you can have one now?"

She shook her head. "My brain already feels like day-old oatmeal. Could I have some more water please?"

As Greg held the cup to her lips, he couldn't help but marvel that Jill's eyelashes were so long and thick. Her normal color was also returning, so she didn't look as pale as she had the day before. He had forgotten that her eyes were such a deep shade of blue; the color of rich cobalt, he decided. And her mouth; did it always look so moist and inviting? He also noticed the taut thrust of her breasts against the cotton of her hospital gown when she shifted in the bed.

Greg gave a mental shake of his head. If he had been without a woman for several months, he could have understood his wandering thoughts. But he had no excuse. Jill was a business partner, and he wasn't going to think of her as anything but. Due to their living and working relationship, it had to be.

Jill was doing a bit of thinking on her own at the same time. She couldn't help but look at Greg's hand as he held the glass for her. The fingertips were slightly blunt, but she knew they had to be sensitive. Soft-looking black hairs finely coated his arm and fingers. A gold ring that resembled an ancient medallion adorned the third finger. She could remember the day he had bought it; she had been with him. The same with the Rolex watch strapped to his wrist; a gift to himself when they received their first multibook contract. She couldn't remember his eyes ever looking such a soft shade of gray as they did now. Her lashes lifted, and she found him gazing at her in an intense way.

Greg's lips twitched. He hadn't missed Jill studying him and then blushing when she realized he saw through her. Funny, he didn't know women could still do that.

Jill lay back, exhausted by her few movements.

"You'd better get some rest," he advised, suddenly feeling guilty for tiring her out. "I'll be back this evening."

"I need some of my things," she said drowsily. "How can I be tired? I've had some very long naps in the past twenty-four hours."

Greg smiled as he watched Jill's eyes slowly close.

Her breathing was deep and regular. He stood and bent over to drop a kiss on her forehead. He was certainly seeing a different picture from the Jill he worked with everyday.

An hour later Greg used his key to open Jill's side of the large house and walked through the living room into the bedroom.

Inside Jill's bedroom he found her carry-on bag near the door and emptied the contents on the bed. He was sure Mrs. Hathaway, the housekeeper they shared, would be willing to clean up in here.

It took some searching for Greg to find Jill's nightgowns in the dresser and a suitable robe in her packed closet. Greg raised his brows at the sight of the filmy French-cut bikini panties and bras that were nothing more than teasing wisps of lace, not to mention other sexy pieces of lingerie. If he had only known her grubby jeans or shorts with oversize sweatshirts covered these tasty bits, he would have looked at her with different eyes during their working day! He plucked her cosmetic bag out of the pile of dirty clothes on the bed and threw it back in the suitcase, along with the nightgowns and robe. He zipped the case closed and carried it downstairs to the large rooms that had been converted into their combined offices and a conference room.

Framed book covers of Hairy Harry's Adventures filled one wall, and various toys of the famous gorilla adorned several shelves along another wall. While the book covers stated the author's name as Tilly Cook, she was really Jill Blake and Greg Richmond. There were times when Greg and Jill alike weren't too fond of the hapless gorilla, but they weren't about to complain about the sizable royalty checks that rolled in twice a year, not to mention the subsidiary rights fees, thanks to cartoon featurettes on Harry's adventures that were syndicated on cable television and toys that had come out two years ago.

Greg called their agent to give an updated report on her progress and suggested that their editor be contacted, since they would require a later deadline for their next book.

He dropped into his desk chair and stared at the blank computer monitor sitting on the computer table adjacent to his large desk.

He couldn't help thinking back over the past five years, the time he had been working with Jill. Their main joke was who would act as Tilly and who would go by the name of Cook the few times they made public appearances at writing conferences or booksellers' conventions.

Someone as rugged-looking and masculine as Greg didn't look like an author of children's books, although it was something he had always wanted to do. The time he had spent at his job as a statistician for an insurance company hadn't been as rewarding as the evening hours, when he had worked on his writing. While his job hadn't been rewarding, it had paid the bills. But, as his agent, Carlysle, had explained to him, the trouble was that while Greg's plots had been strong and well written, he had no gift for dialogue and characterization. The agent had suggested that Greg meet one of his other clients, who had a gift for creating lovable characters and enchanting dialogue but dismal plot lines. Greg and Jill had met one evening for dinner, discussed their ideas, and ended up talking far into the night. Their partnership had blossomed immediately, and their first Hairy Harry book had hit the bookstore shelves eighteen months later. Harry had turned out to be so lovable and appealing that it hadn't been long before he expanded into other areas.

Two years ago Jill had found the house they now lived in and had fallen in love with it. She had had to do some fast talking to convince Greg to see it, but when he agreed, she had excitedly explained her idea to him. Living across town from each other had hampered their writing time, not to mention raising their phone bills when one of them got a brainstorm at an odd hour. It wasn't long before Greg had found himself shopping for the best interest rates for a mortgage, and Jill had talked to contractors about her plan for dividing the huge Victorian house. Even then he had thought to show her how many books they would have to sell to pay for their new home. She had blithely informed him that as long as both their families and friends wrote those cards and letters saying how much they enjoyed Hairy Harry, their finances would be in the black in no time.

The finished product had been admirable, and a testament to one of Jill's earlier jobs, when she had been a secretary for a well-known interior design firm. Street-level garages housed Greg's Volvo and Jill's Trans Am, with stairs leading to the first floor that had the two offices, a greenhouse and spa, and a small conference room where they could work together in comfort. Each office reflected its owner's individual taste. Greg's desk was an old-fashioned rolltop with each cubbyhole filled with papers. His computer terminal and telephone were the only modern features in the room. Jill preferred a modular desk specially built for her computer equipment. Each terminal was hooked into the other so they could share their ideas while remaining in their respective offices if they wished. Separate stairways in the back of the house led to their individual living quarters.

Upstairs, Greg's apartment reflected his love for antiques. While only a thin coating of dust might be found on the light teak in Jill's rooms, it wasn't unusual to find a clean pair of Greg's shorts behind a sofa cushion or an empty beer bottle standing on top of his chest of drawers. His untidy nature endeared him to women as they hovered over him, tidying his mess between his housekeeper's weekly visits. One thing Greg would admit was that he never lacked for feminine companionship. Truth was, Jill never had that problem where men were concerned, either.

Greg suddenly thought of Cal, Jill's latest boyfriend. Funny, he had figured the friendly neighborhood stockbroker would be someone permanent in Jill's life, but it obviously hadn't worked out. He wondered why she hadn't been more upset. The fact that she hadn't mentioned the breakup to him was the reason behind his silent questions. Jill had certainly been distraught when she and Josh Chandler had broken up a year ago, but even then she hadn't discussed the man with Greg. After Greg had looked at her puffy and red-rimmed eyes for a week, he had been sorely tempted to blacken both of Josh's eyes. To this day he hadn't learned the reason for their split and doubted he ever would.

Greg yawned. He still needed to catch up on his sleep. He checked the answering machine, decided none of the messages was urgent, and retired upstairs for a short nap. He did stop long enough to call Jill's mother and report her progress. Knowing how the fluffy-headed woman would be on the first plane if she thought her baby was in danger, he chose his words carefully. He knew Jill wouldn't appreciate having her mother show up for a long stay. Greg had met Louisa Blake once, and that meeting had been more than enough to convince him that the no-nonsense Jill had to have been adopted. If Louisa showed up now, he didn't doubt that Jill would take her ire out on Greg—in a most unpleasant manner.

Upstairs, he stepped over slacks, shirts and underwear scattered on the nut brown carpet and walked into the bathroom for a quick shower. Fifteen minutes later he was stretched out nude on his bed, but sleep didn't come right away. For a brief few seconds the memory of Jill's breasts pressed provocatively against the pale blue hospital gown teased his senses. He laughed and accused himself of being overtired. He still hadn't questioned why he hadn't felt bad about losing Rita. She certainly had been one of the most experienced and creative lovers he had had in his bed in a long time, but there were also times when he felt just a bit empty when they finished their lovemaking. The trouble was, he didn't know why he thought he was missing something. Rita certainly had everything needed for the perfect affair, as had Janis, Suzanne, Marie and a few others. In the next moment his love life was whisked out of his mind and he dropped off into a deep sleep.

CHAPTER TWO

Jill wasn't as lucky. Her mother called later that afternoon and demanded to know just how serious Jill's condition was. The older woman was afraid that Greg, "who is such a sweet boy," had kept something from her when she had talked to him earlier. It took Jill twenty minutes to assure the distraught woman that there were no complications from her surgery and no, she wasn't lying about her condition. Yes, she'd make sure Greg kept Louisa informed on Jill's progress. Louisa mentioned letting Lora, Jill's sister, know about the surgery, but Jill talked her out of it. She was positive that her man-hungry sister was uninterested in her well-being.

Jill smiled weakly at the nurse who came in to leave a tray of small bowls containing her dinner.

"This is so exciting." Jill's tone of voice indicated otherwise as she gazed at broth, gelatin, lemon sherbet, juice and hot tea. "A lousy way to lose weight."

"Ha! As if you needed to lose any," Gloria, her nurse, teased her.

"When do I get some solid food?"

Gloria smiled that bland smile all nurses seemed to use when a patient asked them a pertinent question. "When the doctor says so."

"Then hopefully Dr. Simmons will take pity on me soon." She yawned. "I probably haven't slept as much since I was a baby."

"It's good for you to sleep. It helps the healing process," she assured Jill. "Enjoy your dinner."

"Yeah, sure," Jill muttered, deciding to tackle her sherbet first since it was beginning to melt.

She ate her dinner watching the late-afternoon soap operas, something she had never had the time to do before. Jill became so engrossed in one particular program that she was afraid she was hooked and would want to watch it every day! She doubted Greg would appreciate her taking a half-hour off each afternoon to watch television.

After Gloria took away Jill's tray, she helped Jill with her first trip to the bathroom, showing her how to raise the head of the bed and roll her legs over the side to aid her in getting out of bed. As the two women talked, they were unaware of Greg standing in the hallway.

With Gloria's arm around her shoulders, Jill gingerly stood, only to have her legs almost give out.

"*Augh!*" Jill breathed, closing her eyes against the fire climbing up her legs. She sat back down abruptly, not seeing Greg's expression of alarm and movement toward her. She was too busy fighting the agony in her legs to notice anyone nearby. She turned to Gloria, who stood by patiently. "Look, I don't really need to go just this minute. If you have anything to do, I can wait. No problem." She smiled ruefully, seeing the brief smile in Gloria's eyes. "Okay, I get the message. Let's try it again." She gritted her teeth against the hot needles piercing her leg muscles as she slowly made her way to the bathroom and later back to her bed. "When did the bathroom get moved so far away?" she panted, as Gloria finally settled the covers over her.

"Don't worry, it will get easier each time," the nurse assured her.

"Sure, if my legs don't fall off first."

Greg waited in the hallway until Jill was settled before entering the room.

"I see you've lost some of your apparatus," he greeted her. "You'll be happy to know that I brought you some nightgowns and a robe," he told her, taking the articles of clothing out of the suitcase and hanging them up.

"Greg!" Jill's eyes widened as she watched one peach-colored lace confection spill from his hands. "There is no way I can wear that here."

He shrugged, a broad grin on his face. "I wouldn't object."

"The occupants of the cardiac care unit sure would." She couldn't help laughing over his mock leer.

"Then I guess you don't want this one either." He pulled out something pink and very sheer.

By now Jill's eyes were as large as dinner plates. "Put it away, Greg," she ordered. "Better yet, *throw* it away."

"I found this at the very back of your drawer," he commented a little too innocently. "You sure don't take very good care of your things, Jill. Look how crumpled this is."

"I knew I should have thrown that out," she said through gritted teeth, looking at the not-so-appropriate birthday gift from one of her friends. "Will you put it away before someone comes in?" She had already decided she'd kill him after she felt better.

Instead he held the sheer scrap of fabric up to the

light. "These shoulder straps don't look right," he remarked. "Is that why you don't wear it?"

Jill closed her eyes, wishing she worked with a little old lady who wouldn't have dreamed of digging out something so indecent.

"Those aren't armholes, Greg." Each word was coldly punctuated.

Greg turned the gown around and studied the next-to-nothing front with more than polite interest. "Amazing," he murmured. "One of your boyfriends had very strange taste." He carefully folded the tiny gown and put it back in the suitcase, which was incongruous considering he had originally stuffed her clothes into the case without regard to wrinkles. "I guess you'd prefer wearing this gown, then."

Jill laughed, then groaned at the reaction from her strained muscles as Greg pulled out a long flannel gown that was as prim as the other gown had been improper. "Obviously you had trouble making up your mind."

He hung up the rest of her gowns and placed an emerald green velour robe at the foot of the bed. Her bag of toiletries went into the bathroom cabinet.

"I also brought you some books and magazines." He placed those on the table near her bed. "And someone to keep you company." He placed a large, honey-colored teddy bear next to her.

"Oh, Greg, I love him!" Jill squealed, reaching for the bear. "He's adorable. Thank you." She beamed, hugging the furry bear. "Your flowers came this morning, after you left. Thank you for those, too."

Greg glanced toward the ornate floral arrangement sitting on the counter where a small sink and cabinets were situated.

He smiled. "Just a few more to add to your collection." Unthinking, he brushed a loose curl from her cheek. For a moment the tawny strands clung to his fingers as if they were alive, and he stood there staring at the hair that resembled fine silk against the pillow. He had some brief, wild thoughts about his writing partner as he looked into her deep blue eyes and down to the minute birthmark near the left-hand corner of her lower lip. Milliseconds passed as he wondered how she would taste. He stood there, unaware he resembled someone in a deep trance.

"Greg?" Jill looked worried by his unearthly defection. She snapped her fingers in front of his face to bring him back. "Come in, Greg. So help me, come back or I'll buy you a year's supply of Hairy Harry cereal!" This was her best threat, since they both had tried the honey-flavored breakfast food and decided pancakes and sausage were more in their league.

Greg blinked once and returned to the present.

"It's about time," Jill grumbled, wincing when she shifted her position.

He stiffened. "Are you in pain? Do you want me to call the nurse?"

"I'm fine," she assured him. "These stitches are already beginning to itch and they're driving me crazy. Dr. Simmons must have gotten an A in needlepoint in medical school. Oh, would you do me a favor and call Cecilia and cancel my nail appointment?" She wrinkled her nose. "I have an idea that my nails will be ragged before I can get in to see her. Her card is in my phone file. And please call the dance studio and tell them I'll be out for a while. I

31

would also appreciate your bringing me my cigarettes."

Greg shook his head. "Nope. It will do you good to try a bit of abstinence."

Jill chuckled at that. "Funny, I never thought abstinence had anything to do with smoking."

Greg stayed for two hours, when Jill shooed him out, insisting he call up one of his lady friends and go out for dinner. She told him she wasn't about to ruin all his free time. He vacillated over her suggestion until the phone rang and it turned out to be one of the men Jill had dated not long ago. He couldn't believe that news could travel so fast. Not wanting to stick around and listen to her laugh and talk with another man, he returned home. But Greg didn't call anyone. Instead he heated a frozen dinner in his microwave oven and spent the evening wondering why he was suddenly becoming so interested in Jill. It couldn't be because both of them were suddenly on their own and Jill was now in a vulnerable position. Or could it?

"Talk about gorgeous." Gloria rolled her eyes expressively as she gave Jill a back rub that evening. "How can someone look so sexy and write children's books? In fact, how can you concentrate on your own work when you have someone like him around the office?"

Jill smiled, used to people's surprise that such a good-looking man wrote books geared for young children. "I guess he does look more like the author of men's adventure books or soft porn." She half-turned when the thermometer was carefully placed between her lips. She turned her head slightly to watch the decimals on the square case Gloria carried first climb rapidly, then slow until the instrument read ninety-nine degrees. "That thing reminds me of filling up at the gas station."

Gloria laughed. "That's a pretty good description." She dropped the thermometer sleeve into the wastebasket and reached behind the bed for the blood pressure cuff. Ten minutes later she left, saying she'd be back later with Jill's sleeping pill.

"Terrific. I hope you realize I wouldn't be able to sleep without it," she grumbled, settling back under the covers.

The next morning Jill's first visitor was Dr. Simmons.

"I don't see any reason for you to keep your stitches any longer," he said, walking into her room.

"Those are the second best words I've heard yet," Jill told him.

"What are the best?"

"You telling me I can go home." She smiled.

"Not just yet, young woman." The gray-haired man carefully moved the covers aside and removed the dressing. Jill lay back, waiting for the first snip, and almost jumped when what she felt was the doctor pulling at her abdomen with steel pincers. "Ouch! Hey, what are you doing?"

"Hold out your hand." He dropped a tiny piece of curved metal in her palm.

"A staple?"

"It's called a Michelle clamp," he explained, continuing with his torturous extraction.

"Ow!" she yelped. "Okay, that's it, no more," she ordered. "Just leave the rest in. I won't mind a bit."

"You'd look pretty funny," Dr. Simmons teased without pausing in his work.

"Who cares? It will be a great conversation piece." She gasped at the next pinch.

33

"And you'll play havoc with airport metal detectors, too," he joked.

"Have a heart," she pleaded.

Dr. Simmons held his hands up. "All done, and it wasn't as bad as you made it seem."

"Fine. I want to be around when you have these things in you," Jill grumbled, but there was just the barest hint of a smile in her eyes. "And I want to be the one to take them out."

"You can start walking now," Dr. Simmons informed her. "In fact, you'll find that you'll feel a lot better once you get around more, but don't overdo it." He smiled. "I'll see you in the morning and we'll see how well you're doing."

Jill spent the morning reading one of the books Greg had brought her and keeping an eye out for him. She didn't want to admit that she was looking forward to seeing him. She could say that anyone would do to keep her from going crazy, but deep down she knew better.

Contrary to her expectations, she was soon engrossed in her book and didn't sense another presence in the room until a small stack of envelopes floated down into her lap. She looked up and smiled.

"I hope you left the bills at home."

"Are you kidding? That's all I could find," Greg replied.

Jill read each card and handed a few to Greg. One especially had her chuckling.

"I didn't know they made dirty get-well cards," she commented, still giggling over the sexy message inside the card. "Where did Janine find it?"

"Beats me." He handed the card back to her. "How are you feeling? I'm glad to see that your color is back."

"My color is back due to my screams when Dr. Simmons took my staples out," she groused.

Greg shook his head, not understanding. "Staples?"

"I guess the price of silk thread went up, because he used some very nasty metal clamps instead." She held her pillow against her chest as she coughed. "And I thought having the flu was bad." She pushed the pillow to one side, then pointed to a tall box that resembled a meter. "Good old Respiratory Therapy brought it up this morning," she explained. "I'm to blow into it to keep my lungs clear." She wrinkled her nose in distaste. "I didn't realize there was so much work involved in getting well.

"Carlysle called this morning to see how I was feeling." She smiled at the memory of the slightly eccentric man who represented them with the skill of a viper. "I think he was just making sure I was still alive. He alluded to the fact that you could do all the typing for a while," she said with a teasing grin. It was a fact that neither of them liked to type, so they shared the task, since they preferred going over their work from beginning to end instead of hiring a typist.

Greg's smile didn't quite reach his eyes. He couldn't miss how Jill occasionally winced when she moved and how she bit her lower lip the one time she unconsciously tried to stretch her body. Yet the stubborn witch wouldn't admit she hurt!

"I'm still not used to my limitations," she said with a sigh, reaching out to grasp his fingers. "Greg, I really appreciate you staying with me so much, but I feel guilty at taking so much of your time when I'm sure you'd rather do something else."

His eyes twinkled. "Such as picking up my dirty clothes?"

"I don't know. If you went that far, poor Mrs. Hathaway might have a stroke from the shock," Jill said. "If it wasn't for her and your present girl-friend, I doubt you'd find your furniture for all the clothes scattered everywhere."

"Okay, I get the message." He shook his head. "Hey, shouldn't you be walking by now?" Even he was surprised by the time he had spent with Jill, since he usually wouldn't spend more than five min-utes in a hospital unless he happened to be the patient. Now he was hesitant about leaving Jill alone. He picked Jill's robe up from the bed. He smiled at the blue challis print flannel gown with lace edging the collar and cuffs. Her emerald robe had the same Old World look.

Jill wrinkled her nose in distaste. "You have got to be kidding! Do you know how long it takes me just to walk to the bathroom? It was bad enough that I had to call the nurse every time I needed to get out of bed."

"And now you have me." Greg dropped the robe over Jill's head and zipped it up. Her slippers were next placed on her feet.

"My legs still wobble," she cautioned him.

"Then it won't look funny if you hang on tight," he said lightly, grasping her hands. "Come on, the exercise will do you good. This may be the only time you'll get any."

"Sadist," she muttered under her breath, stand-ing up slowly, still feeling off balance. She gripped Greg's hands tightly, afraid she'd fall without his support. At least the prickles in her legs had less-ened. "Haven't you read the reports that say even a

36

person who jogs on a regular basis can have a heart attack?"

"Just take your time," Greg prompted quietly, sensing she was talking to hide her fear of collapsing.

"I don't need to walk, you know," she argued, taking her first step. "I'll be doing plenty of it for the next fifty years."

Greg's smile curved his lips. "Dr. Simmons said you need to walk, so we'll take a nice stroll down the hall." He kept one arm tucked securely around her. With his head bent, he could smell the light scent of her cologne. Today her hair was twisted into a loose knot on top of her head.

"This happened at the wrong time," she lamented, trying to ignore the tingling sensation along her calves and thighs as they slowly made their way out of the room.

"I don't think emergency surgery can be planned according to your social calendar." Greg's attention was diverted by a shapely red-haired nurse who walked past them.

For the first time in their partnership Jill felt a twinge of jealousy that Greg looked at other women the way a man studied a woman he was interested in while he barely glanced at her. This feeling was new to her, especially since they had taken each other pretty much for granted during the past five years. She also knew it wasn't a feeling she should have. She silently resolved to start livening up her social life as soon as she was free to get out on her own. If she took it easy, she was positive she could be back to her old schedule in a couple of weeks.

Their walk along the hallway was leisurely as they spoke about inconsequential subjects. Anyone who looked at them would think they were an old married couple; Greg's arm was looped protectively around Jill's waist, and she leaned familiarly against him.

When they returned to Jill's room fifteen minutes later, they found four people waiting there.

"Darling, you don't look sick at all!" A woman with jet black, wildly styled hair and equally wildly shadowed eyes exclaimed. She held out her arms, draped in vivid fuchsia dolman sleeves, and embraced Jill.

"Hello, Sofia." She greeted the woman with a smile and flashed Greg a wry expression at Sofia's theatrics.

Greg rolled his eyes in disgust. He wondered if he could ask a nurse for the use of an oxygen tank so he wouldn't have to smell the strong jasmine perfume Sofia used. He felt suffocated from the many heavy scents mixed in the small room and irritated by the noisy talk and laughter.

"Give her a chance to get back in bed," he ordered curtly. "In case you've forgotten, Jill had major surgery only two days ago." He scowled at the two women and two men who had all been talking at once.

Sofia's brightly painted lips pursed. "Jill, dear, how could we forget?" she cooed, stepping back to allow her to reach her bed. The woman's dark eyes spewed hostility in Greg's direction. From their first meeting the two had disliked each other; Greg, because he felt Sofia used Jill unfairly, and Sofia, because she knew Greg saw her for the heartless soul she was.

Greg remained in the doorway feeling split in two directions. He wanted nothing more than to get away from Sofia, but his other half urged him to remain to ensure that Jill's thoughtless visitors wouldn't overtire her.

Jill smiled and thanked them for their flowers and cards. At the same time she couldn't help looking over at Greg. He had made no bones that he wasn't fond of some of her friends, especially Sofia and Drake.

Sofia was the epitome of a bohemian artist. The woman of indeterminate age painted pictures that were nothing more than splashes of nauseating color on canvas that commanded a great deal of money.

Drake was in his forties, with no visible means of support save a family trust fund that more than covered the cost of his elaborate parties and bar bills.

Taffy—the name was incongruous for a woman in her mid-thirties—and Ray were nothing more than hangers-on.

Jill didn't count them as true friends or even close acquaintances, but they had helped brighten her life during some dark periods. She looked at Greg, silently pleading with him to understand.

"I'll see you tomorrow, Jill." His speech was harsher than he intended.

She parted her lips to object, but the cold expression in his eyes told her he wasn't going to give in.

"All right," she conceded quietly. "Thanks for coming by."

"Don't worry, Greg, we won't overtax the dear." Sofia's lips were slightly curled back.

"I certainly hope not." He turned away before he said words he wouldn't regret.

For the first time in many months Jill found herself not enjoying the foursome's eccentric conversation, interspersed with malicious gossip about mutual friends. She felt tired and found herself wishing to be alone. After a while she used the excuse of experiencing discomfort, and they left with promises of seeing her again when she was discharged. Ten minutes later Jill had to call the nurse and ask if she could be given something for the pounding headache that she had received from the loud talk that had surrounded her.

That night Jill took the sleeping pill the nurse had brought in to her and was ready to turn out her light when the phone rang. She quickly prayed that it wasn't her mother and picked the receiver up.

"Hello?"

"They didn't overtire you, did they?"

Jill smiled at the crisp sound of Greg's voice. "The only person who overtired me was myself," she admitted, feeling she would be better off not to tell him about her earlier headache. "I then had a quiet dinner comprised of strained soup of an unknown variety, vanilla ice cream, orange gelatin and hot tea."

Greg chuckled. "Not even a candy bar for your sweet tooth?"

Jill gave an unladylike snort. "Hardly. Oh, could you do me a favor? The copy of *Killers in Orange* is missing five pages from the ninth chapter. Would you mind picking up another copy? It's frustrating to get to a good part and be left hanging."

"How you can read that gore and not have nightmares, I'll never know. Okay, I'll get another copy. I have a luncheon engagement, so I won't be over until the afternoon."

"With Rita?" she asked before she could stop to reconsider. "I hope you didn't get down on your knees to ask her to take you back. It's so demeaning."

He could sense the broad smile on her lips. "Shouldn't she call to beg me to take her back?" he retorted. "Good night, Jilly Bean."

Jill groaned. A former boyfriend had christened her with the whimsical nickname and, unfortunately, Greg had not only heard it once but used it when he wanted to get a rise out of her. She hung up without saying another word.

She switched on the television with the remote control button, pleasantly surprised to find one of her favorite horror movies being aired. She settled back to watch and later, when she fell asleep, dreamed of a dark-haired man carrying her into a mist.

Greg stepped over a softball mitt lying in the middle of the living room and walked into the bedroom. He carried his glass of hearty burgundy into the bathroom and set it on the counter while he took a long hot shower. When he later got into bed, his damp towel was discarded next to the bed and the half-filled wineglass placed on the nighttable next to a glass that had held juice that morning. He looked around the cluttered room and knew that Mrs. Hathaway would mumble more than usual when she cleaned his rooms the next day.

He pushed two pillows behind his back and reached for his glass. Greg decided it was time to question his sanity. He had worked with Jill in pretty close quarters for the past five years, and now was not the time to think about her seriously as a desirable woman.

Greg knew enough about Jill's private life to know that men found her an exciting woman to be with. He had met some of the men she had dated over the years when they had stopped in during the

41

day to take her to lunch. A few times she didn't return all afternoon, but he had never thought to question her about how she spent those hours, just as she never had the times he had been gone.

Greg sipped his wine, wondering why his and Jill's love lives never seemed to bear the right kind of fruit. He couldn't remember either of them finding someone who could change their minds about the single life. Jill had thought she found someone in Josh, until something happened to break them apart, and after that she didn't seem to care about seeking a man who wanted commitment.

He set the glass to one side and promised himself to take his dirty glasses into the kitchen before Mrs. Hathaway arrived in the morning.

Rubbing his hand over his face, he suddenly grinned, remembering Jill's sounds of surprise when he mentioned he had a luncheon date. He hadn't informed her that his engagement was with his accountant, but the thought of the lovely Marcia would only have heightened Jill's suspicion that good old Greg was on the prowl again. He pulled the covers over himself and settled down to a good night's sleep.

"Why can't I go home today?" Jill demanded of the tolerant Dr. Simmons. "My temperature has been normal for two days, I'm eating this horrible food you're serving me, and I'm behaving so well the nurses probably think I'm nuts!"

He shook his head. "It's much too soon, Jill. And you forget that your temperature still fluctuates during the day. You're also not as strong as you think you are. You're going to be severely restricted for six weeks."

"Six weeks!" She had been certain she would be

returning to full activity in a couple of weeks. "You can't do this to me," Jill pleaded. "Please, let me go home. I promise to be good."

Dr. Simmons shook his head again. "Not yet. As it is, you'll have to be careful because you'll have to climb stairs. You will have to make sure you go up and down as little as possible. I would prefer that you only travel the stairs once a day. I also don't want you driving for ten days after you get home."

"How am I supposed to get around?" Jill demanded.

"I'm sure Greg will drive you anywhere you need to go," he assured her.

Jill sighed, seeing this was one battle she wasn't going to win. "When *do* I get to go home?" she asked quietly.

"In two days, if all goes well." Dr. Simmons patted her hand. "Just relax and enjoy this unexpected vacation."

"Vacation?" She made a face. "My idea of a vacation is a beach bungalow in Hawaii."

"Then you're in luck." He beamed. "Your room has a terrific view of the bay." With that he walked out of the room.

Jill glared at his retreating figure with as much venom as she could muster in her weakened condition. "Smart-aleck doctors do not deserve to have their bills paid right away," she muttered, picking up a magazine.

But the magazine couldn't hold her attention for long and she finally gave up, hoping a walk along the hall would curb some of her restlessness. Jill slipped her robe and slippers on and walked slowly, occasionally smiling at a nurse or one of the other patients who obviously had had the same idea.

She stopped at a set of windows but couldn't see

much of anything due to the low-hanging fog that refused to dissipate. Jill pressed her cheek against the cold glass and looked out into the gray mist that resembled Greg's eyes. She wished she had been bold enough to ask Greg whom he was having lunch with. Would it prove to be one of those afternoon-long meals, or was it business? She shook her head, deciding her preoccupation with Greg was due to her semi-invalid state. She needed something to focus her overactive imagination on, and who better than Greg, with the many women who enjoyed cooking meals for him and straightening up his cluttered rooms?

Jill's brow wrinkled in a frown as she silently scolded herself for thinking about him so much. It always seemed that the times she was between boyfriends, Greg had had someone to keep him busy, and when he had been free, she had had someone in her life; they were never on their own at the same time. Perhaps it was for the best, she thought. Or was it really? Were they better off keeping their relationship purely on a business basis? Jill guessed that she'd never really know.

She finally straightened up and returned to her room, deciding to call her friend Janine and have a lengthy chat on the phone. Janine suffered from a strong phobia of hospitals and found it next to impossible to walk into one without breaking out in a cold sweat. Jill respected that fear, and the two women had kept in touch over the phone during the past few days. Janine had already promised to see Jill once she returned home. But her friend wasn't home, and Jill's spirits did not improve. Finally she opened her book and began reading again. Every time she turned a page, she checked her small travel clock sitting on the nighttable. Time had never passed so slowly.

CHAPTER THREE

Jill felt far from cheerful when a smiling Greg walked in, still carrying the scent of the damp air from outside. She didn't have to look at her clock to know it was past four. She had glanced at it when she heard his voice out in the hallway as he spoke to one of the nurses.

"Obviously you had a successful lunch," she said.

Greg grinned. "Sorry, I was never one to kiss and tell." He dropped into the nearby chair, his dark eyes twinkling with humor. "Marcia chose a German restaurant that opened recently. You'd like it."

"Marcia." Jill looked as if she had bit into something sour; she knew the woman only too well.

"She's a nice woman," Greg told her.

"I'm sure they said the very same thing about Lizzie Borden." She collapsed back against her pillow. "I'm sorry, Greg; I've been feeling cranky all day." She thought that sounded like an excellent excuse for insulting a woman she didn't like anyway.

He looked down at his hands in his lap. "It's probably your inability to get out as much as you're used to," he murmured. "I understand one of your favorite boutiques had to declare bankruptcy this morning. It's amazing what can happen with the loss of just one patron."

She wished she had the energy to shake her fist at him. "Cute, Richmond, real cute."

Greg dug into his jacket pocket and drew out a square package. "Your book—with the ninth chapter intact."

Jill smiled her thanks. "It was very frustrating to read that the general was killed but not by what method."

"I'm sure his murder is as gory as the cover suggests." He shook his head in wonderment that someone who looked so sweet and fragile would read such grim books. "How can you stand to read them?"

Jill's eyes sparkled. "There was a great horror movie on TV last night; ghouls and plenty of vampires." She raised her eyebrows expressively. "Not to mention other nasty creatures of the night. I loved it."

"I didn't know Sofia had made a movie," Greg commented with a straight face.

Jill's laugh escaped before she could stop it. "Come to think of it, there was one witchy type who reminded me of her." She ran her fingers through her hair, enjoying the clean feel of the strands. "I was able to take a shower today and it was wonderful! I didn't know I could get so excited about taking a shower."

"Depends on who you're taking it with," he murmured.

Jill put her hands over her stomach as she laughed. "You're getting terrible!" she accused, but her laughter took the sting out of her words. "I swear your depraved nature is showing more and more."

"Must be the company I keep."

"True, Rita did look a little on the kinky side," she replied with a straight face.

Greg's visit continued with the same lightheartedness on the surface, but there was something else occurring between them, perhaps because they were both aware that they were free agents at the same time. From the beginning of their partnership they had been aware that they found each other attractive, but it was an unspoken agreement that a love affair just wouldn't work for them if they wanted to keep their business relationship on an even keel. For five years it had worked—until now. The tension hanging between them was unusually thick when Greg left.

Jill was ecstatic the morning Dr. Simmons announced she could go home. In her excitement she barely listened to his instructions and the reminder to see him in a week's time.

"Now, no going to your dance class for quite a while, young woman," he cautioned, wagging his finger at her.

"No problem there," Jill assured him airily. "The way my legs feel right now, I don't think I could try a plié without falling flat on my face."

She had already called Greg and was waiting for him to pick her up. The details concerning Jill's discharge turned out to be more complicated than her admittance. It seemed to take hours before an aide finally wheeled her out to Greg's car, with her flowers set in an accompanying basket.

During the drive to the house Jill discovered that hills and a sore stomach didn't mix. By the time Greg helped her into the house, she was fully prepared to hate him for life. She was also positive he had hit every pothole and found every bump during the trip.

"Too bad you didn't hit Lombard Street so my insides could end up a total disaster," she grumbled, then yelped when Greg suddenly swung her up in his arms. "What are you doing?"

"Making sure you won't moan and groan every step of the way."

Jill linked her arms around Greg's neck before she could lose her balance. She had never been in such close contact with him, save for casual kisses, and she discovered it wasn't so bad. She could smell his aftershave, which reminded her of the woods after a cleansing rain, and found their faces close enough so that she could see a faint red speck where he must have nicked himself shaving that morning. For one brief moment she was sorely tempted to nibble on his earlobe, but she resisted the urge.

"You're showing your romantic side, Greg," she teased lightly, tugging on a lock of his hair with an ungentle hand. "My, my, is this what you do with all your lady friends? It must have been difficult with Rita, since she's a bit"—she paused dramatically—"topheavy."

"If you weren't sick, I'd drop you on your lovely tush," he retorted, carrying her into her bedroom, where the covers had already been pulled back. Greg set Jill down on the sheets and put her suitcase on the cushioned chair. He pulled the infamous peach nightgown out and held it up. "Would you like me to help you slip into this?"

"No, thank you, I think I can handle it all by myself," she cooed back. "Besides, I thought your forte was assisting women *out* of their nightgowns, not into them."

49

"True, but in your case I'd force myself to do the proper thing," he said with a smirk.

"You probably haven't done the proper thing since you were in kindergarten," Jill retorted. "Now if you want to help me, I'd appreciate a pitcher of ice water."

Greg nodded and left the room. He came back a few minutes later carrying a tray laden with a pitcher, a glass and a plate of butter crackers. He set it on the nighttable and looked down at Jill. "If you need anything, give a holler," he told her. "We got the galleys yesterday for our spring book, so I thought I'd begin going over them."

"I'll proof them," Jill offered instantly, knowing it wasn't one of his favorite jobs.

"You don't worry about a thing; just rest," he replied. "I'll see you later."

After Greg left, Jill changed into a nightgown— not the peach one—and wandered into the living room. She curled up in a corner of her muted rose, ecru and turquoise plaid couch and sorted through her mail. As the rest of the day passed, the time moved rapidly, between reading her mail and talking to friends on the phone. Before she knew it evening had come and her stomach reminded her that the dinner hour had come and gone. The passing of the day had also sapped what little energy she had, and she was finding it difficult to combat her lethargy to go and search for some food when someone knocked on her front door and opened it.

"Ready for some dinner?" Greg asked.

Jill pursed her lips in thought. "Dinner, dinner," she mused. "Oh, I guess you can stay long enough to drop it off."

"Too bad, because I come with the meal." He entered carrying red and white cardboard boxes that sent out the enticing aroma of chicken. Jill's mouth watered.

"I'll get the plates," she offered instantly, starting to rise from her corner.

"No way." He shook his head, setting the boxes on the coffee table and proffering a paper bag that held a package of paper plates and plastic eating utensils.

Jill's lips twitched. "I see you brought your best china. How considerate of you."

"Only quality for milady." He opened the cellophane wrapper and withdrew two heavy plates with a yellow scrolled design along the border. "Even spaghetti sauce doesn't leak through these." He loaded each plate with chicken, coleslaw and biscuits and handed the smaller portion to Jill. "Do you want root beer or uncola?"

"Uncola." Jill was still amazed at the feast he had brought.

Greg pulled a package out of his jacket pocket and tossed it onto the glass-topped teak coffee table. "I also got your prescriptions filled."

By then Jill was speechless. "I forgot all about those," she murmured, opening the bag to find two bottles, one filled with painkillers and the other with sleeping pills. "Thank you. I can see that between the pain pills and sleeping capsules, I'll be out of commission for the next month."

"If they work that well I'll gladly take care of refilling them for the rest of this year," he offered blandly, getting up to find glasses and ice for the cans of soda.

"Honest to goodness solid food," she said, drooling theatrically. "Greg, I can actually chew this!" She picked up the chicken and bit into the juicy meat.

51

Silence reigned for the next ten minutes as they concentrated on their meal.

Greg looked around the spotless room. "Did Mrs. Hathaway come in today?"

Jill's eyes bugged. "Do you mean you've already messed your place up so much you can't remember what day she's at your place and when she's at mine?" she demanded.

He winced. "The woman hates me," he announced. "All she ever does is mumble and give me dirty looks."

Jill nodded her head, understanding what he meant. Their sour-faced housekeeper always mumbled when she was displeased with something or someone—usually Greg and his less than immaculate habits. It wasn't that he was a slob; he was merely careless with his possessions.

"She's probably working up to demand a raise from you," she decided. "I certainly wouldn't blame her. After all, you give her three times more work than I do." She curled her legs up under her but winced at her movement.

Greg noticed her silent admittance of the pain crossing her abdomen and reached for one of the pill bottles, working to open the safety cap. "I once saw a cartoon of a man walking out of a drugstore where a boy stood nearby wearing a sign saying he'd open childproof bottles for a quarter. I could use that kid right about now," he grumbled, reading the embossed directions on the top. It took a bit of struggling, but he finally got the lid off. He dropped one of the white tablets into his palm and handed it to Jill. "I'll get you a glass of water."

"Now I know what a bowl of lumpy oatmeal feels like," she muttered, accepting the glass, then popping the pill in her mouth and drinking some of the

52

water. She looked at the food she had really picked at more than eaten. "I usually would have eaten this in no time."

"Your stomach is still adjusting from your liquid diet in the hospital," Greg explained, swiping her drumstick. "No use in letting it go to waste" was his reply to her questioning gaze. When he had finished he cleaned up the remains of their meal and deposited the trash in the proper place. When he completed his task, the coffee table was as clean as before.

"Hm, you just might end up as a human being after all," Jill quipped.

"Be careful or I won't show up to fix your breakfast tomorrow morning," he threatened.

"Mrs. Hathaway is coming in early," she announced smugly, not wanting to hurt his feelings by reminding him that he could never cook breakfast without burning at least one item. "She called this afternoon and said she would check on me."

Greg choked, remembering the one time the housekeeper had fixed a meal for him. It had taken his stomach several days to recover. "I guess you'll have your pick of two bad cooks. Good night, ole buddy." He leaned down to kiss her on the cheek. "You have an early night and get your rest."

"I thought that was what I've been doing," she said.

"It's still going to take you awhile before you feel more like your ornery self."

"What an exciting prospect." Jill looked grumpy.

"I'll see you tomorrow," Greg promised.

After he left, Jill picked her book up and continued reading. An hour later she retired to bed. For someone who rarely went to bed before two or three in the morning, the clock reading just past ten mocked Jill's weary eyes.

Even with her early bedtime, Jill slept until late morning. When her bedroom door closed, the sound of Mrs. Hathaway vacuuming was merely a pleasant hum. She rubbed her sleep-filled eyes with the heels of her hands and staggered out of bed into the bathroom for a quick shower.

Under the warm spray she looked down at the incision and grimaced. Dr. Simmons had assured her the pinkish red scar would fade within a year or so. For now she knew what Frankenstein's monster felt like.

Jill braided her damp hair and left it hanging down her back as she slipped on a pale gray sweatshirtlike caftan edged with bright turquoise on the round collar and cuffs. Since she felt that she still appeared too pale, she brushed a rose blusher across her cheekbones and used a matching lip gloss. Now that she felt a bit more human, she walked into the living room, where Mrs. Hathaway was busy polishing the furniture.

"Good morning, Mrs. Hathaway," Jill said sweetly.

The tall, angular woman turned around to fix Jill with dark, beady eyes. She was in her fifties and looked as if she continually sucked lemons, but she was a hard worker and trustworthy.

"You'll need some breakfast," Mrs. Hathaway said in her characteristic mumble.

"I can fix something," Jill protested politely.

"You sit there and rest," she ordered. "I'll be back in a jiffy with your meal."

Jill discovered that Mrs. Hathaway's poached egg was just another name for hard-boiled, and her buttered toast had a delightful charcoal coating. Jill forced herself to smile as she swallowed every bite along with sips of pulpy orange juice.

"That's better," Mrs. Hathaway decreed, carrying the dishes into the kitchen. "Before I go I'll fix up a casserole for your dinner."

"*No!*" Jill almost shouted, then got herself in control. "That's very nice of you, Mrs. Hathaway, but Greg said he'd be bringing dinner over." She was afraid her smile would break before long.

After the housekeeper left, Jill spent the afternoon ensconced on the couch watching television or reading. She couldn't remember the last time she had been blessed with so much free time, although she doubted she would consider it a blessing for long. She was surprised to find herself not even thinking about Harry and his travels. As it was, she found it difficult to concentrate. Janine called her for a long chat and promised to stop in as soon as she could. Carlysle also called to see how she was getting along. Surprisingly, there was no word from Greg. During one of her prowls around the living room she looked out the window but didn't see his car parked in the driveway.

The hours dragged slowly for Jill as she found herself with virtually nothing to do. That evening she was eager to greet Greg when he brought up dinner for them. She was so happy to see him that she didn't even mind his teasing her about Mrs. Hathaway's disastrous breakfast.

For the next few days Jill was restless, but not quite strong enough to leave her apartment. Thankfully, Janine, her vibrant friend, came over one afternoon to visit, armed with a gallon tin of caramel corn, a two-pound box of chocolate-covered marshmallows with a caramel base and a six-pack of strawberry soda. The combination sounded nauseating, but it had always been one of their favorite snacks in college.

"This will probably make me sick," Jill decided, but that didn't stop her from digging into the candied corn.

Janine idly studied her long, scarlet-painted nails. "If all that glop in the hospital—not to mention Mrs. Hathaway's deadly cooking—didn't kill you, this certainly won't," she pronounced with a shake of her dark curls. "How is your gorgeous writing partner taking care of you?"

"Just fine." Jill opened a can of soda. "He's been nice enough to curtail his busy social life to bring me dinner and even lunch a few times. He also stops in to check on me a couple of times a day, and he'll be taking me to the doctor tomorrow."

"Honey, he's acting more than nice," Janine hooted in her slow Southern drawl. "That guy has always had the hots for you." She laughed, noticing Jill's puzzled expression. "Don't play dumb with me, sweetie pie. That man wants to jump on your bones—bad."

Jill's eyes widened to deep blue saucers at her friend's blunt statement before she burst into unrestrained laughter. "Now I know you're not playing with a full deck. Greg is too busy with his various ladies." She shook her head. "For once, my friend, your sixth sense is way off."

Janine gave her a rapid denial. "I am never wrong," she declared haughtily.

Jill rolled her eyes. Janine's gift of sensing episodes in the near future was an accepted fact between them, even when it caused problems.

"Remember that time we went skiing over Christmas vacation? I still say you rigged that slope to dump me," Jill accused good-naturedly, chewing on a rich piece of candy.

Janine remembered that time only too well. She had told Jill to stay off a particular slope when Jill had left that morning to ski with friends. Unfortunately, Jill didn't listen and ended up breaking her leg.

"Everyone knows how much you hate to be wrong," Jill told her.

"How can I hate something I've never been?" Janine's dark amethyst eyes sparkled. One hand pushed the tousled curls off her nape. With her perfect features and ivory skin, she looked as if she should be a model instead of a professional makeup artist. She was a free-lance consultant, working in various department stores doing makeovers and demonstrating the proper way to use the high-priced cosmetics. Janine's professionalism had earned her the right to pick and choose her jobs, and if she wanted to, she wouldn't have a single day off that year.

"Then I wish you had told me about Dr. Genet's propensity for coeds." Jill brought up an old argument.

The dark-haired woman chuckled. "No way. After all, you were there for an education, and he certainly wanted to give you one!" The two women choked with laughter at the reminder of the lecherous psychology instructor from their college days.

Jill and Janine had met in college, when they were assigned to the same dormitory room. They had hit it off instantly and were inseparable from that time on. Janine had been so blasé regarding her second sight that Jill soon accepted her friend's tendency to move off into another world as simply an everyday

57

occurrence. They left the University of Arizona with degrees in English and struck out in unrelated fields. Jill soon discovered that her typing and shorthand skills found her more jobs, but her need for challenges couldn't keep her interested longer than six months. She used to laugh, stating that no one else could have the lengthy résumé she did. Writing was the only area where she felt happy and comfortable, since it presented her with a new challenge every day.

Janine studied Jill with her usual intent gaze. "I found a good hairstyle for you in a magazine I was glancing through the other day," she commented. "All you need is about six inches cut off and the remaining hair permed. You'd never have to worry about all that weight when you wash it, and the drying time would be minimal." She nodded. "Yes, I can see you in it."

Jill groaned. "Just like the time you could see me in that black dress for Sheila's party? The people who didn't know me thought I was a hooker!"

"Call girl," Janine corrected her. "And you were the hit of the party. What more can you ask for? Think about all the men who called to ask you out."

"Sure," she responded. "And I bet I could have made a fortune to replace the unearthly amount I paid for that dress. I haven't worn it since."

Janine stayed for another hour, then explained she had to leave to get ready for a date. She paused at the door.

"Don't let first impressions disappoint you," she told Jill, a tiny smile tugging at the corners of her lips as if she was privy to a humorous secret.

"What?" Jill frowned, not understanding her remark.

Janine's smile widened. "Some things are just

better the second time around." She blew Jill a kiss and left.

"What are you talking about?" Jill hurried to the top of the stairs, but her friend merely waved and bounced out the door. "Janine, come back here and explain your mumbo-jumbo!" She flushed when Greg appeared at the foot of the stairs. Jill was suddenly aware of her tousled hair, apricot caftan and bare feet.

Gret looked up and felt his mouth go dry. Jill might have looked disheveled, but she also looked incredibly sexy.

"Having a slumber party?" he asked finally, wincing at the stupidity of his question.

Jill grinned, now back on familiar footing. "Slumber parties last all night and tend to have more than two people."

"Not the ones I've been to," he countered, turning away. "They never had more than two people."

Jill returned to the living room, puzzled by the abrupt change in Greg. She also remembered the look in his eyes when he gazed up at her and wondered if his expression has been what she thought it was—desire.

Greg walked back into his office and sat down. He braced his elbows on the chair arms, his fingers forming a steeple, the fingertips pressed against his lips. He found it difficult to forget the alluring picture Jill had made standing at the top of the stairs. His writer's brain told him she was the perfect image of a woman waiting for her lover, and his overactive imagination told him what would happen once the two lovers closed the door behind them. He groaned silently, cursing the suddenly tight fit of his jeans.

Greg's brows drew together in confusion. More

and more he was thinking of Jill as a desirable woman with delectable curves, bedroom eyes and hair the color of tawny silk. This was not something he could continue thinking about and still manage to work with her successfully. What had brought about the abrupt change? Sure, they had always been aware of each other in the physical sense, but they also knew that that kind of attraction could prove dangerous. Maybe that was why they always made sure to have someone around to keep them occupied. Greg wondered if this wasn't a good time to make up with Rita.

He shook his head and turned to the computer with the dark screen that silently mocked him. He decided it was as good a time as any to begin plotting the next book.

Early that evening Jill paid dearly for her food orgy with an old-fashioned stomachache. She lay in bed loudly asking when death would come to take her away.

"I hadn't realized I had been renamed," Greg called out. He stopped in the doorway, then hurried into the bedroom. "Jill, what's wrong? Is it your incision?" he demanded, dropping down on one knee beside the bed. "Talk to me or I'm calling the doctor."

Jill managed a weak smile. "He'd only tell you to give me an Antacid and call him in the morning."

"Give it to me in plain English," he insisted.

She closed her eyes. "It's a combination of strawberry soda, chocolate candy and caramel corn."

Greg groaned, but not in sympathy. His expression clearly said that Jill fully deserved what she got. "No wonder you've got a whopper of a bellyache. I'll get you something for it." He got up and went into the bathroom to rummage through the cabinets until he found what he was looking for. He handed Jill a glass of the fizzy water and helped her sit up to drink it.

"After all the sugar you consumed, you'd better get some protein into your system."

"I don't want to look at food," Jill moaned.

"Like it or not, you're going to have to eat something a bit more healthy than you previously had." He left the room quickly.

Jill lay still, waiting for the seltzer to take effect. She wished she had told Greg that eating would just make her sicker. He soon returned carrying a tray with a bowl and a small plate on it.

"Cream of chicken soup and soda crackers," he announced. "I also cut you a small piece of cheese for you to nibble on first. That should help your stomach."

Jill took several experimental bites of the sharp cheddar until she realized her stomach wouldn't revolt before attempting to finish the slice. She had to admit it did help and felt ready to tackle the soup. Greg had also made her a cup of hot tea and sat in the nearby chair while she ate her dinner.

Jill found the warm soup comforting to her abused stomach, and the bowl was empty before she knew it. She declined seconds, deciding she wasn't going to tempt fate.

"Don't you realize you're poisoning your system eating all that junk food?" Greg remonstrated.

Jill shrugged, feeling more confident now that her stomach had settled down. "I remember you making a large dent in the fruitcake I made at Christmas, and it didn't seem to affect you," she reminded him.

"I didn't sit there and eat the whole thing."

"No, just half." She smiled sweetly.

Greg exhaled a sharp breath of frustration. "Jill, you can't afford to put further stress on your stomach muscles. Getting nauseous from junk food is pretty stupid." Jill wrinkled her nose in disgust. He glanced down at his watch. "I'm meeting someone in an hour for dinner, so I'd better start getting ready. Do you need anything?"

"No, thank you." Jill hesitated, unsure whether to say what was foremost on her mind. She decided to go for it. "Greg, are you and Rita back together again?"

Greg thought about the fast talking he had had to do to persuade her to go out with him again. He knew that what had truly changed her mind was the mention of Maxwell's Plum, an exclusive restaurant with prices to match the decor. What she didn't know was that he planned to have a long talk with her regarding her cryptic words on the night of Jill's surgery.

Jill saw the strained expression in Greg's eyes and easily guessed the identity of his dinner partner.

"Have a nice dinner," she told him, wishing she could tell him he could do so much better than the alluring Rita. The trouble was, she doubted he'd listen to her. She lifted her eyebrows comically. "Give me all the gory details tomorrow. Also, don't forget my doctor's appointment is at eleven."

"You don't have to worry; I'll be here," he promised. "Good night, Jilly Bean."

I could kill Randy for coming up with that ridiculous nickname, she thought, glaring at Greg's retreating figure. She slumped under the covers, looking as if she was going to spend the rest of the night pouting, but that wasn't her style. It wasn't long before she remembered the book she had been reading earlier and that she had just gotten to a good part. Soon she was engrossed in the story of a forties-style private detective searching for his girlfriend's killer. Jill didn't want to stop to think that she was also wondering what Greg would be like as a date.

Greg was bored. Considering how desirable Rita looked in a clinging wine wool dress and with her hair combed in a sleek knot, he still found it difficult to keep his attention on her, and she knew it.

By the time they entered her plush high-rise apartment, neither person looked very happy.

Rita poured two measures of brandy and handed one to Greg.

"I've been offered a promotion on the East Coast, effective after the first of the year," she announced without preamble, seating herself in the pale gray plush chair adjacent to the burgundy couch where Greg was seated.

He looked up with surprise. "Is this for the vice-presidency?"

Rita nodded, sipping her brandy. She was presently head of the marketing department of an international computer firm, and her dream of the vice-president's office seemed finally to have come true.

"I'm glad for you, Rita," he said sincerely, aware of how much the promotion meant to her.

Her smile was deadly. "I'm sure you are, in more ways than one." A manicured nail circled the rim of her glass. "Perhaps you'll finally see the light, so to speak."

By now Greg's patience had come to an end. Rita's sly comments had dug into his skin all evening, and he was determined to find the cause for them. He set his glass on the chrome and glass coffee table, then swiveled to face Rita. "What the hell do you mean by that?"

For a brief moment regret dimmed her eyes. Then a stronger emotion took over as she steeled herself to say the words that had been eating at her for weeks. She didn't hesitate before speaking.

"It's quite simple, really. I'd say that each time you make love to me, you're actually making love to Jill, and I'm sure you were the same with your other women before you met me. In fact, I wouldn't be surprised if she doesn't do the very same thing. The time has come for both of you to face the facts and become lovers." After she dropped her bomb she sat back, waiting for the fallout to settle.

CHAPTER FOUR

For the longest time Greg sat on the couch staring at Rita. He found himself unable to come up with a scathing retort or think of one word that would be appropriate to the situation. If he cared to be honest with himself, he wouldn't bother arguing with the truth. He mumbled an excuse, escaping as quickly as possible. He noticed that Rita didn't try to persuade him to stay.

Instead of returning home Greg headed for a nearby pub owned by an old friend of his and Jill's.

Since it was near closing time, Mahoney's was almost empty of customers. A burly-looking man with bright red hair streaked with gray cropped close in a crew cut and a pair of blue eyes to rival Paul Newman's greeted Greg with a brief wave of his hand before filling two steins with beer and handing them to the waitress.

"Long time no see." He walked the length of the bar, expertly mixed bourbon and water, and set it in front of Greg. "What'cha been up to?"

Greg sipped his drink, allowing the alcohol to warm his throat and stomach before he spoke. "I had to rush Jill to the hospital with a hot appendix ten days ago. I've been playing nursemaid since then." He took another sip of the potent drink.

John "Tank" Mahoney saw the new signs in Greg's manner, the same way Rita had.

"That's a duty I sure wouldn't turn down." His voice was gritty from too much whiskey and too many cigars. His broad, homely face showed a wide grin. The moment Greg finished his drink, a fist the size of a small ham grabbed the glass and refilled it, this time with more bourbon than water.

"Damnit, Tank, she's more trouble than she's worth," Greg grumbled, not sure if he was talking about Jill or Rita.

"All broads are trouble," the large man pronounced before shouting out, "Last call, people! The bar closes in ten minutes."

Greg sat at the bar nursing his drink while Tank set up the last drinks ordered.

The bar had no band, only a jukebox with records from the forties and fifties. There were no plush booths offering privacy to the customers, only plain wooden tables and chairs. The walls were decorated with foreign battle flags and photos taken during World War II and the Korean War. When Sergeant Major Mahoney had retired after thirty years in the Army Tank Corps, he was determined to have his own bar. His dream had been fulfilled, and the pub was well known for the excellent liquor served and no trouble allowed. No one was about to tangle with a man who more than resembled his nickname and, when thwarted, displayed the temper of a wounded grizzly bear. Over the past few years Greg and Jill, semi-regulars in the bar, had become good friends with the crusty-natured man.

Twenty minutes later Tank locked the front door and returned to the bar, where Greg stood still nursing his second drink. The older man shook his head at the sight of his friend's morose features.

"Why don't you just bed the broad and have done with it?" Tank suggested, drawing himself a beer and downing it quickly.

The younger man grimaced at his blunt words. "I don't think Rita would appreciate being called a broad," he countered mildly.

"Who's talking about Miss Big Business?" Tank shook his head at Greg's stupidity. "I'm talking about Jill. She's the one who's been giving you trouble since day one, if you'd care to admit it. Hell, anyone with brains could see the broad's got the hots for you as much as you do for her. What I can't understand is why neither of you won't do anything about it. She's sure more woman than some of those female robots you go out with." Tank felt he had the right to an opinion, since Greg had brought many of his woman friends into Mahoney's for a drink. Tank had later let him know he didn't think much of any of them. He pushed even further. "I bet she's one hot little number in the sack."

Greg's lips tightened at the thought of a few of Jill's former lovers. Tank didn't miss his reaction.

"That's the worst way to ruin a good friendship and excellent business relationship," Greg muttered, unwittingly admitting the many times he had thought of Jill in a much more personal way.

"If you believe that, I've got a bridge out in the bay I'd like to sell ya." Tank shook his head, amused with the logic of Greg's argument, which left nothing open for typical human behavior. "Buddy, you don't share a house with a doll like Jill and not fantasize about how she'd be in bed. If you don't do that, you're sure not normal."

Greg smiled at Tank's sharp observation. He hated to admit it, but there were times when an erotic fantasy would take over without any warning.

It was pretty easy to do when he and Jill shared late-night snacks or breakfast with robes as the dress code. How many times had a tousle-headed Jill entered Greg's kitchen dressed in her favorite silk kimono which barely covered the essentials, and how many mornings had he shown up at her place to find her wearing nothing more than an oversize T-shirt? How had he remained sane all this time?

"You still goin' with that dame with the big—"

"Nope," Greg answered swiftly. "Rita and I parted company tonight."

"Is Jill still seeing the Wimp of Wall Street?" Tank clearly believed in speaking his mind.

Greg chuckled, since he had seen Cal in the same light. "No."

"So what's holding you back now?" The large man demanded. "Get outta here!" The smile in his eyes took the sting out of the order that bordered on a drill sergeant's roar. He shook his head briskly when Greg reached into his pocket to pay for his drinks. "I don't accept payment after hours. Go home."

When Greg arrived home he was surprised to find Jill's bedroom lights still shining. A typical night owl, she was known to stay up until dawn reading one of her gory murder mysteries, only to show up for work in the morning bleary-eyed and out of sorts. Greg had often teased her, saying she probably couldn't go to sleep after reading one of her favorite thrillers. He hadn't expected her energy level to resume so soon after her surgery.

In the comfort of his bedroom it didn't take him long to undress and fall into bed, only to have some very erotic dreams starring Jill and himself.

The next morning, when he had returned from his run, Greg found a note from Jill tacked on his door reminding him of his promise to take her to the doctor that morning.

Promptly at ten o'clock a freshly showered Greg appeared at Jill's door and escorted her down to his car.

"I don't see why I have to see Dr. Simmons again," Jill complained during the short drive to the medical center. "I feel fine. This is really a waste of time."

"He just wants to see for himself how well you feel," he told her, pulling into the parking lot.

Luckily Jill's wait wasn't very long and the examination was even shorter. Dr. Simmons told her he was proud of her fast recovery but also warned her against overdoing her activities.

"And no dancing just yet," he reminded her, wagging a finger at her.

Jill nodded, not wishing to ruin her recovery when it was so far along.

"It sounds like you're well on your way to returning to your usual crazy self," Greg told her as they walked back out to the parking lot.

"Thank goodness." She blew out a breath of relief. "Oh, I forgot to ask how your date with Rita went last night." When Jill saw the thunderous expression on Greg's face, she could have pinched herself. "Forget I asked," she muttered, looking down at her feet.

Greg continued walking, unable to forget Rita's accusations and hating to admit that her words were more than a little true.

Jill noticed the bleak expression in Greg's eyes and figured Rita had to be the cause. In the hope of cheering him up, she smiled and looped her arm through his and hugged herself against him.

"It appears we don't have the best of luck with

the opposite sex, old boy. Don't worry, I won't throw you to the wolves."

Greg halted so abruptly that Jill would have fallen if she hadn't been holding on to his arm.

"Do me a favor, just worry about yourself for once," he snapped, his dark features threatening an upcoming storm. "Damnit, Jill, can't I have any privacy in my life without you pushing in to give unwanted advice?" He jerked open the passenger door and practically pushed her inside.

Well aware she had said too much, Jill remained quiet during the drive back to the house until a shop facing the street caught her eye.

"Stop the car!" she commanded.

"What?" Greg almost slammed on the brakes, looking wildly at his passenger.

"There's the cutest sweater in that boutique over there. Can you find a parking space so I can check on it?" Jill asked.

Greg counted to ten. "You almost give me a heart attack because of a lousy sweater?" he shouted. "I thought you had lost something valuable. Why couldn't the doctor have taken out your buying tendencies along with your appendix?"

"Please?" she wheedled.

He sighed heavily. "Okay, there's a spot over there. Just do me a favor, will you? Don't make up for lost time. This car can only hold so much."

Jill did make up for her time away from the stores by buying two pairs of pants, a shirt and three dresses along with the infamous sweater. Greg gave thanks out loud that it wasn't his credit card getting the workout.

The next day Jill argued with Greg that she felt well enough to resume work on their new book. In fact, she was more than ready to do something to relieve a great deal of the energy stored up in her body. She promised to be downstairs the following day, ready for work.

Promptly at ten-thirty, Jill's idea of the beginning of a workday, she appeared in the doorway of Greg's office.

"Good morning," she greeted him cheerfully.

He looked up and groaned at the sight of bright red parachute pants, oversize gray sweatshirt and worn black ballet slippers. Her hair was pulled back in a careless ponytail, and she was happily munching on a candy bar.

"One, morning is almost over. Two, how can you stand there eating candy so early in the day?" Greg demanded.

With a shrug of her shoulders Jill entered the office and perched herself on top of the worktable beside Greg's desk.

"This has everything breakfast cereal has." She motioned with the peanut, caramel, chocolate, and nougat concoction. "It's known as instant energy food, according to the ads. How are the ideas for the new book coming along?"

Greg shook his head. "Not at all. We need to come up with a new angle. Have any ideas?"

After Jill finished her candy bar she settled herself in a cross-legged position on the table. She dusted her hands off and tossed the crumpled candy wrapper into the wastebasket with a shot guaranteed to turn any basketball player's eyes green. "Story conference time." She smiled prettily. "Let's see, what shall we have good old Harry do this time?"

Greg leaned back in his chair and propped his feet on the desk. Jill slyly studied the length of jeans-clad leg from hem to waist and found everything to her satisfaction. She hid her smile as her thoughts continued wandering along the same vein until she sternly brought them back to serious business.

An hour later Greg was engrossed in fashioning a chain of colored plastic-coated paper clips. Jill was busy applying a bright coral shade of nail polish.

"Why don't we have him run for president?" Greg spoke up.

Jill thought for a moment, then shook her head. "It sounds good, but maybe we should wait writing one like that until an election year."

"How about him taking a train trip?"

She didn't even look up from her task. "We did something similar two years ago."

"He could visit the circus." A bright red paper clip was hooked onto a green one as the chain trailed down to the gold tweed carpet.

"Nah." She replaced the polish brush in the bottle and carefully screwed the top shut. She held up her nails, studying them carefully. "I'm going to have to make an appointment to get these done. They're really a mess."

"He could rob a bank." Laughter sparkled in Greg's eyes.

"Cute, Greg, real cute. Parents would love us showing their kids how to pull off the perfect heist."

Greg straightened, snapping his fingers when his hot idea sprang forth. "I've got it! He'll climb the Empire State Building!"

Jill shot Greg a wry look. "It's been done."

He shrugged as if it was no matter. "Okay, hotshot, come up with something better," he challenged.

Jill smiled sweetly. "He can visit Santa Claus at

72

the North Pole." One shoulder rose daintily in a coy gesture of triumph.

Greg's brows knit together in concentration as he thought over her suggestion. "He could help make the toys, whip the elves into shape and perhaps even substitute for Rudolph on Christmas Eve. It just might work, and it could come out for Christmas a year from now."

"Of course it will work." She replied, insinuating that there was no doubt her idea was pure genius.

"Okay." Greg pulled a box of computer diskettes out of his desk drawer and inserted one in the second disk drive; the other drive held the word processing software. He flipped the terminal on and typed in a few commands. "How's he going to get up to the great white outdoors?"

Jill leaned her chin in her cupped palm. "Perhaps he wants to tell Santa in person what he wants for Christmas?" She leaned over and rummaged in a nearby drawer. "What happened to the candy bar I left in here?"

"You probably ate it."

Greg typed with the time-honored system of hunt and peck. He sighed, hoping Jill would take pity on him and do the typing, but she was too engrossed in hunting for her candy bar and throwing out suggestions for him to type into the rough outline they would start with. Actually she was purposely ignoring his plight. She was well aware that if she gave in to him too often, she'd end up doing all the typing, and she had suffered through too many temporary jobs involving heavy typing to get caught in that trap again. Thanks to Greg's skillful maneuverings, she had typed the entire manuscript of their first book. She had learned her lesson after that.

They worked on the outline until mid-afternoon,

before breaking for a late lunch of chicken salad sandwiches at Jill's place. Greg added an apple to eat with his sandwich and Jill added a slice of blueberry pie to her lunch.

"I think we have another winner," she decided, finding Greg's face much more interesting to look at than her pie. She continued to study him under the cover of her lashes.

"Do I have something on my nose?" Amusement laced his voice.

Jill squinted, carefully dissecting every microscopic inch of his face. "You nicked yourself shaving," she diagnosed finally. But she found it difficult to ignore the strange feelings coursing through her veins as a result of her careful investigation of Greg's face. "You seem to do that a lot. Perhaps you should use an electric razor."

He looked at the large calendar on the wall near the refrigerator, with the many notes she had jotted in the large boxes

"How long will you be out of your dance class?" he asked absently, watching her carry the dishes to the sink, rinse them off and place them in the dishwasher.

"Six weeks," she replied, wiping her hands on a dishtowel, carefully folding it and draping it over a nearby towel rack. In a matter of minutes the kitchen was sparkling clean. "The trouble is, we're having a performance in a couple months, and I'll have a great deal of catching up to do when I return to class." She spooned the last of the chicken salad into a plastic container and placed it in the refrigerator.

"Guess you better pack your tutus in mothballs so nothing happens to them before you return to class." His dark eyes danced with amusement.

"You should talk. Some of your athletic clothing isn't all that great to look at." She stuck her tongue out at him.

Greg sprawled in the chair, laughing at Jill's return to childhood. "How about dropping over to Mahoney's tonight for a couple of drinks?" he invited.

"Janine's coming over." She turned away, not seeing the disappointment flicker across his face.

"She could come along." His invitation was half-hearted.

Jill turned back, laughing at the scowl he wore. "Oh, Greg, don't sound so grumpy," she chided, walking over and looping her arms around his neck. "Tell you what—why don't we go down to Fisherman's Wharf for lunch tomorrow?"

"Damnit, Jill!" he rasped out. "You don't have to treat me as if I'm some kid who has to be pacified!"

Jill stood back, stunned by yet another display of bad temper from a man who rarely raised his voice. Generally Greg was the most even-tempered man she had known, which was the opposite of her own volatile nature, but lately he had been very edgy.

"She really got to you, didn't she?" she asked in a hushed voice that couldn't quite mask her sorrow.

"What are you talking about?"

"You're upset over Rita dumping you," Jill clarified.

"Your surgery seems to have badly impaired your brain."

At his nasty comment Jill felt tears fill her eyes, an experience she wasn't accustomed to.

"I just wish I knew what I did to make you so angry with me, Greg," she sniffed, wiping at the tears with the back of her hand. "I don't know why you persist in yelling at me all the time, but I do

75

know I don't like it." Due to her tears, her eyes turned a liquid midnight blue.

"Jill, give me a break," Greg begged, taking her into his arms and cradling her against him. "You know I can't handle it if you start crying."

"But why are you acting like some kind of crazed monster?" she sobbed, linking her arms around his waist.

"I don't know, babe." He sighed, nuzzling the soft silk of her hair. "It's just been a bad few days for me."

"Maybe so, but you're not being fair to me. I still don't feel good, and crying hurts my stomach." She unconsciously snuggled closer to him. "This is all your fault."

Greg never felt so helpless as when a woman cried. It was even worse listening to Jill, since she wasn't a woman to use tears to break down a man's defenses. All he could do was gently rub her back and croon soft words in her ear until she calmed down.

At the same time he was acutely conscious of the strawberry fragrance lingering in her hair from her morning shampoo and the light floral scent of her perfume. He was also aware of her breasts pressing warmly against his chest and her hips cradled intimately into his. He clenched his teeth when he felt the heated stirrings begin deep down in his body.

"Jill, are you okay now?" It took all his self-control to sound normal, but he had to get away from her before his arousal became known.

"No." She sniffed, pulling away. "My face is red and blotchy, my eyes are swollen and I have a headache."

He chuckled at her complaint, grateful that the tension left his body before Jill noticed it.

"Mahoney's tomorrow night then?" he asked. Jill nodded. "Why don't we go over the outline in the morning to smooth the rough edges? That way you can rest this afternoon and be ready to go in the morning. That is, if you can manage to push yourself out of bed before noon," he ended on a teasing note.

She made a comical face. "You are so funny."

"Yeah, such a great guy, too." With that he sauntered out of the kitchen and out of the apartment.

But Jill wasn't laughing. It wasn't the first time she had seriously considered taking one of his outrageous remarks at face value. There was no doubt about Greg's good looks. He certainly had enough adoring women to prove it. Jill had often commented that no woman in her right mind would want a man who thought living room chairs were meant to hold his laundry, but, surprisingly enough, a majority of his lady friends were more than happy to push aside their liberated status and fold his clothes, iron his shirts and clean up his kitchen in between Mrs. Hathaway's visits. Jill also noticed that none of them ever complained about Greg's less than immaculate habits. She wondered if it had to do with a latent mothering instinct.

She was still pondering her more than usual interest in Greg when Janine arrived, carrying a bottle of white wine and a bag of sugar cookies meant to melt in the mouth. Jill's contribution to their meal was a spinach quiche.

As they later relaxed with their dessert of wine and cookies, Jill spoke aloud some of her thoughts regarding Greg.

"I always knew the two of you wouldn't be able to ignore each other much longer." Janine smirked.

"I'm surprised your pact of just remaining friends has lasted this long."

"Ha! If you think I want to join the likes of Rita, Sheryl, Renee, Ginny, and more other women than I'd care to count, you've got rocks in your head," Jill argued, then groaned when she saw the gleam in her friend's eye. "No, Janine, no more hocus-pocus. I do not want to listen to any more of your predictions."

Janine ignored her. "You're just going to have to be open and watch all the signs," she advised, laughing loudly when Jill threw a small velvet pillow at her. "You can't fight fate, Jill."

"The man has no personal interest in me," Jill protested. "As soon as everything settles down, he'll be out prowling around until he finds someone new to take Rita's place." She didn't find the idea comforting. "Although there won't be much difference in whomever he chooses, since his women all seem to be alike."

Janine raised her eyebrows in a silent question.

"They're all tall, willowy due to careful dieting, but certainly curved in all the right places. They have careers, not just jobs, usually in a professional field, and they know the rules of Greg's game so well you'd think they had invented them," Jill explained. "Meaning there are no ties, and when the time comes to part, they remain friends." She wrinkled her nose. "Greg's accountant, dentist, and hairstylist are all ex-lovers. His past is more colorful than my wardrobe."

Janine chuckled, pulling the last cookie out of the bag, breaking it in two and handing half to Jill. "We should all be so lucky."

"What about Ross?" Jill asked, referring to an attorney Janine had been seeing recently.

Janine shook her head. "He had some pretty strange notions the first time he took me to his apartment."

Jill's eyes grew very round. "Really? But he seemed so nice that time Cal and I met the two of you for dinner."

"Let's just say that a man's apartment decorated in black leather with a medieval dungeon look to it gives me a weird feeling."

Jill chewed on her lower lip, unable to equate the low-key, blond man dressed in the pinstripe suit with someone who obviously preferred leather in the privacy of his home. "It just goes to show you can't trust your first impressions," she mused. "He certainly didn't look the type."

"I should have known something was wrong when he kept asking me to wear my black boots." Janine looked thoroughly disgusted. "Luckily I've worked all those clinics lately, so I'm too busy to care that my current social life is zip."

Jill lay back against the couch and groaned loudly. "Men are one big pain in the neck four feet south," she declared.

"Maybe, but they do have their uses." Janine grinned wickedly, and the two women promptly dissolved into giggles such as they had shared since their years at college.

The following day passed smoothly, with Jill rising at nine to work with Greg on their new outline. She even took the time to dress in pale green linen pants and a matching cable knit sweater. She clipped the sides of her hair back and applied a light coating of makeup. She was all nonchalance when she sauntered into the office.

Greg glanced up, then did a doubletake. A low

wolf whistle escaped his lips. "Don't tell me you're finally giving up those rags you usually wear," he couldn't resist commenting.

"I decided that if you're taking me to lunch today, I should wear something a little more tasteful." She gestured to her outfit with a languid air.

"I should have known you were going to stick me with the tab," he murmured, standing up and pulling out a nearby chair with a courtly gesture. "Milady."

"Thank you, Jeeves." Jill's drawl was definitely upper class English. She sat down, sliding her legs to one side, the ankles demurely crossed. Her lady of the manor routine was ruined when she crossed her eyes.

"Stop that!" Greg's forefinger tapped the tip of her nose. "Someday you're going to do that and you won't be able to uncross those cute eyes of yours."

"I bet I wouldn't have to appear as Tilly Cook then." She laughed. "Carlysle would have a fit, wouldn't he?" She leaned back in the chair, her legs crossed, one foot seeming to tap out a silent rhythm. It was one of the few times she wasn't able to tune in on his thoughts. In fact, it seemed to happen more and more lately. Ironically, it was happening just when she wanted to know even more about him. She watched him, idly noting the knife-sharp crease of his designer jeans and the fit of his spice-colored polo shirt. He looked so good!

"Jill!"

"Hm?" She slowly raised her eyes from the spot where his nipple impudently betrayed itself through the soft knit fabric.

"Clean out your ears, lady," he ordered affectionately. "I've asked you three times if you're ready to tackle the outline."

"Oh, sure." She still found it difficult to rouse herself. "Sounds fine."

Greg wasn't entirely convinced, especially since working on an outline wasn't one of Jill's favorite tasks. She preferred to get right into the heart of the book.

They did get some work done, however, then had a leisurely lunch at Fisherman's Wharf. As was their custom, they flipped a coin to determine if they would sit in the smoking or nonsmoking section of the restaurant. It wasn't that Greg strongly objected to Jill's smoking, even though he gave her a bad time about smoking in the office. It was merely a courtesy they shared. Two hours later they returned home to work some more, and that evening they spent a few hours at Mahoney's.

Jill was amused at Tank's heavy-handed attempts at matchmaking, and Greg was just plain disgusted that a two-hundred-eighty-pound man was acting like Dolly Levi. As a result, he drank more bourbon than usual. The trouble was, he couldn't even get drunk, since Tank didn't allow excessive drinking in his bar and had the muscle to back up his rules.

"If you're so up on togetherness, Tank, why haven't you snared someone of your own?" Jill asked with a smile after he had expounded on the virtue of romance.

He snorted around the cigar in his mouth. "Hell, no. They're too much trouble." He stomped away when someone called out to him.

"Let's go." Greg dropped a couple of bills on the table and took Jill's arm.

He remained morose and quiet during the short walk back to their house.

"Greg, you know that Tank didn't mean any harm," Jill chided him when they reached her front door. "You shouldn't take him seriously. You're perfectly safe from me," she teased.

"Yeah, sure," he mumbled, leaning against the door frame. He straightened, staring at Jill with eyes that seemed to glow a foggy gray in the dim light.

"Sleep tight." She couldn't resist chuckling at her choice of words.

"Smart aleck," he grumbled, reaching out for Jill and pulling her toward him. He kissed her thoroughly before disappearing down the stairs.

Jill remained in the doorway, stunned by the throbbing of her lips and the racing beat in her body.

"Well, I'll be," she murmured, a smile lighting up her face. Things were certainly livening up around here!

CHAPTER FIVE

With the outline of Hairy Harry's new adventure finished, Jill and Greg repaired to their respective offices. Greg would work on writing the general story line while Jill worked up a complete personality sketch on each character. This part of the job usually took them about a week; then they would get back together to merge their thoughts and work together from there on.

A few weeks after Jill's surgery, she dressed in leotards and tried a few stretching exercises, only to learn exactly how tender her abdomen muscles were. She pressed her hands against her stomach as if her touch would force the soreness to disappear. Not in the mood to change her clothes, she walked downstairs to her office still in her dancewear.

"Well, if it isn't Pavlova's successor," Greg greeted her with a steaming hot cup of coffee. He found himself fascinated by the way the crop top of her leotard parted to reveal a silky strip of flesh when she reached for the cup. "In case you've forgotten, the doctor told you no strenuous exercise for six weeks and you've just passed the halfway mark." There was no mistaking the thread of steel in his pleasant tone. What he really meant was that Jill would only be attending her dance class when *he* said so and the doctor agreed.

Jill smiled and patted his cheek. "And here I thought you'd enjoy looking at my legs," she cooed, setting the cup down and striking a sexy pose with her hips thrust to one side provocatively. Her pink, glossy lips pouted and her eyes half closed to resemble a sultry siren.

Greg swallowed. Oh, yes, he was extremely interested in looking at Jill's legs, along with a few other parts of her anatomy. Nothing was difficult to miss in her multicolored leotard with hot pink tights, leg warmers and black leather ballet shoes. He wondered why the stretchy fabric had to reveal the bones outling her slim hips and the shape of her unbound breasts.

"Don't you ever wear a bra?" he complained gruffly, turning away from the enticing sight.

Jill raised her eyebrows in surprise at his question. "I guess I don't feel as if I need to worry, since I don't have the—ah—qualifications ninety-nine per cent of your girlfriends have." She smiled sweetly. "Wait a minute—there was Laura. If I recall correctly, she couldn't even have been helped by a teen bra."

"Jill Blake, you've got a mean streak a mile long."

"Hm, I must be improving. Last time you said it was five miles long." She plopped herself in the chair behind her desk.

For the balance of the morning lazy banter was interspersed with casual innuendoes.

Jill was ready to suggest that they go out for Mexican food for lunch when an unexpected visitor upset the even tenor of their day.

When the doorbell rang, Greg called out that he'd get it. Engrossed in her work, Jill didn't bother to listen to the masculine murmurs coming from the entryway.

"Jill." Greg's voice was tight with some unidentifiable emotion.

"Hm?" She didn't bother to look up from the flickering screen of the computer monitor before her.

"You have company."

This time Jill didn't miss the harsh edge of Greg's words. She turned her head and looked up to see the tall man standing just behind Greg's left shoulder. *Oh no!* Her throat closed, refusing to allow any words to pass between her lips.

"Hello, Jill." The man's voice was the stuff women's dreams were made of.

This time her vocal cords loosened. "Josh."

"I'm sure the two of you will excuse me," Greg said stiffly, his manner indicating he wasn't pleased by Josh's arrival.

"Of course." She refused to flinch under his silent condemnation.

When Greg left the room he made sure to close the door behind him.

"It's been a long time." So sure was he of his welcome, Josh sat in a nearby chair without bothering to ask Jill's permission. For a moment he seemed content to study her with hungry eyes.

"Has it?" She feigned disinterest. Jill wished she could tell herself Josh wasn't as handsome as she remembered, but she knew she'd only be lying. Josh's rich, coffee brown hair was still carefully styled, his tan as deep as ever, and his suit well tailored. He exuded the aura of the successful businessman who wheeled and dealed in Washington, D.C., when not traveling around the country. Jill had fallen in love with him the year before, only to fall from her cloud with a very nasty bump. In the end she cut Josh out of her life as painfully as a surgeon operating without anesthesia, and the agony hadn't ceased easily. In fact, it had taken a long time before she felt like a member of the human race again. Now she sat across from him, silently marveling that she had ever loved such a shallow man.

"Why are you here, Josh?" she asked quietly.

His smile was the result of expensive dental work. "I wanted to see you."

"Why?"

"To take you out to dinner this evening."

"All right." Jill wanted to smile at Josh's quickly masked look of triumph. If he only knew what was in store for him. "You can pick me up at eight." She stood up in a silent sign of dismissal.

"Until then." Josh rose to his feet and sauntered over to Jill, intending to kiss her on the lips. She turned her face at the last moment so that his mouth brushed her cheek instead.

Sensing the success of Josh's visit, upon his return to the office Greg was less than polite to Jill, especially when she informed him that she had a date with Josh that evening. Greg merely muttered that he would be gone for the rest of the afternoon and left the house.

That evening she dressed in an emerald green silk chemise that skimmed lightly over her hips. Greg hovered nearby when Jill opened the front door after the bell rang. She was grateful that Josh was smart enough not to just walk in as he used to do.

"Oh, Jill, don't forget that you can't engage in strenuous activities for a couple more weeks," Greg reminded her coolly, standing near the stairs.

Jill whirled, her visitor momentarily forgotten. "Thank you, Greg." Her low voice tore through him like a partially dull knife. "It's nice to see that you're looking out for me so well." She quickly opened the door and slipped outside.

Josh took Jill to an expensive restaurant and showered her with lavish flattery, but she was unmoved. It was easy for her to beg off going to his hotel for a nightcap, and an angry Josh took her home.

"It wasn't because of me you broke off our affair, Jill," he sneered, watching her alight from the taxi. "The only man who could have all of you is Richmond. It's a shame really, because we could still have a great time if you cared to spread yourself around a bit."

"Good-bye, Josh." She walked up the stairs to the front door without a backward glance.

Still immersed in the past, Jill bypassed her stairs for Greg's. Without knocking, she walked inside his apartment; they never bothered locking their apartment doors. Then she continued through the darkened living room to the bedroom, where a light still shone.

"What the—" Greg sat up under the covers and put the book he had been trying to read aside. "Home early, aren't you?"

"Give me a break, Greg." Jill kicked her shoes off, picked up Greg's glass and took a healthy swallow of his drink. She bent over coughing as the potent alcohol hit her stomach like a fiery sledgehammer.

"Serves you right." Greg leaned over, snatching the glass out of her hand. "There's wine in the refrigerator if you'd prefer something milder. I'm sure you'll understand if I don't get it for you." His eyes flicked toward his robe lying across a nearby chair.

Jill took his advice and went into the kitchen to

pour herself a glass of Chardonnay. She returned to the bedroom to find Greg sitting up in bed, his quilt covering him more securely.

"To a tarnished god," she toasted, holding up a glass.

"Didn't he appreciate being turned down?" Greg couldn't resist asking, already figuring out why Jill had returned home so early.

"Does any man?" She settled herself on the bed against the headboard next to Greg and adjusted the covers around her feet.

"Hey, will you watch it?" he ordered, grabbing the covers back before the cold air hit his naked skin.

"My feet are cold," Jill grumbled, finally hiking her dress up and tucking her feet under her.

"Your damn feet are always cold." Greg wished his robe were closer so he could get up to fix himself another drink. "Would you mind mixing another one for me?" He held up his glass.

She arched an eyebrow. "You can't do it yourself?"

"Not without embarrassing both of us, since I'm not into wearing pajamas."

Jill couldn't resist a wicked smile. "You've seen one, you've seen them all." But she did take his glass and go out to the kitchen to fix his drink. Jill wondered why Greg was acting so embarrassed. As she had told him, he certainly didn't have anything different from other men. Or did he? She stood at the counter, still holding the club soda bottle. She wasn't staring at anything in particular, but her silent question had set her to thinking. What was Greg like as a lover? He had to be good, judging from all his satisfied-looking girl friends. Perhaps that was why his previous lovers remained his friends. Were they hoping to gain admittance to his bed again? Still lost in her thoughts, Jill carried the glass back into the bedroom.

"Here." She handed it to Greg.

He sipped and almost choked on the straight bourbon. "Thanks," he said with a touch of dry sarcasm. He waited until Jill seated herself back on the bed, although he was sorely tempted to suggest that she sit in the chair. He doubted that he was up to any more of her teasing about his "modesty."

"So what happened during your date with Josh?"

Jill sighed. She hadn't told Greg what had happened when she had broken up with Josh, but she knew she would only be really over the man when she aired the truth. "He wants me back and I said no," she murmured, picking up her wineglass and studying the contents.

Greg instinctively knew there was more to the story. "And?" he prompted softly.

Jill grimaced. "I always thought of myself as a very together woman. I make a good living, have a nice house, I'm not all that bad-looking, and I've had my share of men without any complications." She winced at the painful thoughts intruding from her past. "Until I met Josh, that is. As you may remember, I met him at one of Janine's parties and we hit it off right away. He told me he worked for a computer firm in Washington, D.C., but traveled here once a month for three or four days."

Greg nodded grimly, also remembering that he and Josh hadn't gotten along from the beginning.

"Pretty soon we spent all his free time together." Jill drew a deep breath, finding it difficult to continue. "And for the first time in my life I thought about commitments." Her lips twisted in a bitter smile. "Luckily I was shaken to my senses before I made a fool of myself." Her hand trembled as she set the wineglass down and slowly turned to face Greg. "One afternoon, while I was waiting for Josh in the office he used when he was in the city, I took a telephone message from his wife. Luckily she thought I was a secretary, but I still felt like a fool."

"What did he say when you confronted him with your knowledge?" Greg asked.

Jill uttered a harsh laugh. "He assumed I had known all along that he was married. It seemed that he had given me enough hints; I just hadn't noticed them. Or hadn't wanted to," she added under her breath. She silently cursed herself for the hot tears filling her eyes. "It turned out that the bastard had a mistress in each of the other three states he traveled to. I was the California one. Needless to say, I came to my senses immediately and told him if he ever tried to contact me again, I'd call his wife and let her know what he was pulling. It was apparent he didn't want her to know."

"Why did he show up again after all this time?" Greg inquired, wishing he could take her into his arms and give her the comfort she needed.

Jill sniffed. "I guess he figured I'd be ready to take him back by now. Maybe I should have offered to run an ad for him. 'Mistress needed four days a month; experience preferred.' " She choked on the last two words.

This time Greg did take her in his arms. "Poor baby," he crooned, stroking her back. "He really screwed you up, didn't he?"

"He had no feelings for me," she said with a sniff, circling his neck with her arms. She snuggled closer to him. "I'm just glad I found out before I told him how I felt about him."

"He was never for you," he declared confidently,

rubbing his chin lightly over the top of her head. "You're doin' fine, sweetheart, and you've got me to take care of you."

"Ha! With the full social life you have, you don't have the time to take care of a goldfish," she argued, looking up with tear-bright eyes.

He shook her gently. "Have you noticed me seeing anyone lately?" Jill shook her head. "Then I rest my case."

For the next fifteen minutes they sat huddled together. Greg was beginning to regret it, since sharing close quarters with Jill was having a very noticeable effect on his body. He shifted his position, bringing one leg up, his knee bent in an effort to hide his arousal from her.

"Oh, I'm sorry, I'm probably turning you into a pretzel," Jill apologized, unaware of his discomfort. She glanced at the bedside clock. "I'd better get going. Thanks for the comfort." She leaned over and kissed him lightly on the mouth. For a moment she was tempted to kiss him again, but the strange light in Greg's eyes stopped her. "Good night, Greg." Her voice came out husky and all too inviting.

For a long time after Jill left, Greg lay in bed berating himself for letting her go so easily.

The next morning he was up early and jogged until his entire body felt like a piece of cooked macaroni. After he returned home he took a hot shower and drank a couple of cups of hot coffee to lure him back to the land of the living. He was hard at work downstairs when Jill sauntered in wearing a pair of faded tight jeans and a lipstick-red oversize sweatshirt.

Greg leaned back in his chair and eyed her with amazement. "When did they start manufacturing faded denim spray paint?'' He ducked when a paperback book sailed through the air in his direction.

"That's about as nasty as you can get, Richmond." Jill sat on the edge of his desk.

"Aren't you afraid of splitting something?" Greg glanced down at her trim thighs, wondering how she stayed so slim with all the sweets she ate.

"That just might happen if I don't return to dance class pretty soon," she grumbled.

"Oh, come now, you're not going to tell me that doing pliés and whatever else you do burns up enough calories to keep you so thin." His disbelief was obvious.

"It's certainly a lot more fun than a boring run around the same old park every morning." Jill sighed theatrically, unable to resist a few digs of her own. "It's amazing how tights can look so good on a man. They—ah—they show off the best of people, if you know what I mean?" She closed one eye in a sly wink.

Greg knew what she meant only too well, and he didn't like the mental picture he was receiving.

"Of course, male dancers have to be extremely strong," Jill chatted on. "That's so they can easily pick their partners up and carry them."

"Do you want some coffee?" Greg practically shouted, jumping to his feet.

Jill blinked, looking oh-so-innocent. "Yes, I would. How nice of you to ask," she simpered.

That did it. With a glare fit to kill, Greg stomped off. Jill ended up working the rest of the morning by herself.

The next few days continued in the same vein, one of them picking a ridiculous argument that escalated until the other left to cool off, something that had rarely happened before. This morning was not much different when Greg brought up a topic Jill preferred forgotten.

"Do you have any preferences for next Tuesday?" Greg asked, after they finished proofreading the first two chapters.

Jill looked up. "About what?"

"For your birthday dinner. I've already figured I'll be signing over the next three royalty checks to pay for the meal," he told her. "At least that's what you said you'd do to me after you took me out for dinner on my birthday."

"I don't want a birthday dinner," she said quickly, returning to her work.

"We could have a party," Greg mused, unaware of the tension coiled inside Jill. "We should do something special for this particular birthday. How does a party sound?"

"I don't want a party; I don't want to go out to dinner; I just want to spend the day in bed." Her clenched hands lying in her lap was another sign of her agitation.

Greg was surprised by Jill's distraught state. It had been a practice of theirs over the past few years to treat the other to dinner out on birthdays. Then he remembered Janine warning him that Jill's mental state would be off balance for a while.

"It's called post-op depression," she had explained to him one morning when they spoke on the phone. "When she gets upset for no reason, just humor her, but be warned that it may not work. It doesn't hurt to try, though."

"Are you sure you'll want to spend the day in bed?" he asked mildly. "After all, it is a special day for you. If you'd like, we could drive up to Napa and tour some of the wineries."

"*No!*" she shouted, turning on him with the ferocity of a wildcat. "I don't want to do *anything* on my birthday. All it means is that I'm turning thirty, and soon I'll be thirty-five and, well, I don't want to think about what happens after that."

The light bulb went on in Greg's brain. So that was the problem . . . Jill wasn't looking forward to her thirtieth birthday. He had heard that a lot of women dreaded the big three-o. Now all he had to do was figure out how to handle the situation.

"Hey, babe." He laid his arm across her shoulders in a comforting gesture. "Don't you know you're not getting older, you're getting better?" Now that had the right touch.

Jill's unladylike snort told him her opinion of his advice. "Forget it. I don't want to be thirty," she insisted stubbornly. "So if I stay in bed all day, it will go by without me and I won't turn thirty."

Greg was very tempted to ask where Jill got her crazy logic, but he knew better. "Why don't we pretend it's an ordinary day and just go out to dinner?"

She eyed him warily. "What's the reason for our going out if it isn't for my birthday?"

She had him stumped. "It's close enough to Easter; we could celebrate that." He looked very proud of himself for coming up with the perfect solution. "Besides, when have we ever needed a reason to go out?"

Jill didn't look very convinced. "We'll see," was all she would say.

Tuesday morning Jill purposely stayed in bed later than usual. She was glad she didn't have to work that day if she didn't want to because she only wanted to hide away. She wasn't that lucky.

"Meet me for lunch at one o'clock," Janine ordered after listening to the phone ring fifteen times before Jill deigned to answer it.

"I have another appointment," she lied.

"No, you don't. You be at I. Magnin at a quarter to one. I'm holding a clinic there." Janine hung up before Jill could voice another excuse.

"There are times when friends are a natural enemy," Jill muttered, forcing herself out of bed. She staggered into the bathroom and reached up to open the medicine cabinet. Her hand stopped in midair as she studied her reflection in the mirror. She widened her eyes, then narrowed them. She inclined her head closer to the mirror to examine every inch of the skin around her eyes and didn't like what she found. She silently counted the imaginary lines and wrinkles. She then went to work hunting for gray hairs, which were next to impossible to find among the tawny blond strands.

At eleven o'clock a bouquet of yellow roses arrived for Jill. The enclosed card was from Greg, saying he'd pick her up at eight. There was nothing to indicate that the roses were for her birthday.

At ten to one Jill wound her way through the aisles of the cosmetics department until she found Janine.

"Happy birthday!" Janine greeted her with a hug.

"Please!" Jill groaned. "I can't handle this. It is not my birthday. I refuse to allow it."

Janine laughed. "No such luck. Come on, we're having a fattening lunch to celebrate. Is Greg taking you out to dinner tonight?"

Jill nodded glumly.

"Good. I'll do your makeup for you," Janine offered. "When I finish you'll be the new sex symbol."

Over lunch Jill confessed to finding new wrinkles and a couple of gray hairs.

"Pooh!" Janine dismissed her friend's fears with a casual wave of her hand. "If you'd use that new moisturizer I gave you, your skin would feel a hundred percent better. As for your hair, we're taking care of that this afternoon, my gift to you." She froze, looking across the room.

"Earth to Janine," Jill sang out, waving a hand in front of her face. "All right, Janine, get your head out of the outer limits." Her command was laced with amusement. She was only too used to her friend suddenly leaving reality for several minutes.

Janine smiled and returned her attention to Jill. "Take a casual look over your left shoulder. You'll see a man with reddish hair dressed in a blue suit at the third table from the doorway. He's the man I'm going to marry."

A moment later Jill glanced in the direction Janine had indicated. "Mmm, very nice, but he might have a wife and six kids your vibes aren't picking up."

Still smiling, Janine shook her head. "Oh, no, I can feel a recent divorce, but it wasn't anything messy. He's the one."

Jill fiddled with her shrimp salad and took a bite before replying. "Janine, you've finally done it. And if you're not careful, the men in white coats will be here with a designer straitjacket in your size."

"Poor Jill. Even after all these years you still can't understand, can you?" Janine's tone was benign, that of a mother explaining a simple formula to her daughter. "How can you doubt me?"

Jill leaned across the table so no one else could hear her. "Then I think you should join the circus and wear a flowered skirt and a kerchief around your hair. Don't forget the gold chains, because you'll become a very popular fortune-teller. This is just a bit much, unless you've met the man and have forgotten to tell me."

Janine shook her head, not insulted by her friend's words. "No, but I will . . . soon." She looked very sure of herself.

Jill rolled her eyes in exasperation. Instead of continuing her argument, she picked up the carafe of wine and topped off her glass.

"If you pull this off, I'll send the two of you on a fantastic honeymoon," she promised.

"Be careful, I just might take you up on it," Janine teased.

After a calorie-filled dessert of Black Forest cake, Janine steered Jill to her next surprise.

"Oh, no," Jill figuratively dug her heels into the pavement outside a chrome-and-glass one-story building.

"Yes." Janine literally pushed her inside. "Hi, Shari. Is Chad ready?" She smiled at the receptionist, whose gel-encrusted black hair stuck out in deadly spikes with bright green-dyed tips.

"I'm too conservative for this place," Jill whispered, wishing she could tune out the hard rock music assaulting her ears. She sat gingerly on a square black canvas cushion that doubled as a chair. "I'm not going to let some guy with a shaved head work on my hair," she whispered fiercely, watching one tall skinny bald young man. "It's not fair," she moaned, burying her face in her hands. "It's bad enough that I turned thirty today, but to end up *here.*" She glared at Janine. "I cannot stay here and have someone dye my hair plaid or shave it into a mohawk."

"Ms. Blake." A deep male voice poured over her like warm honey.

Jill looked up and used all her concentration to keep her mouth closed and her eyes in their sockets. The man standing in front of her was absolutely gorgeous. Sun-streaked brown hair, stylishly cut, framed big hazel eyes and a perfect nose, while a definitely sensual mouth finished his good-looking face.

"Omigod," she breathed.

"Treat her gently, Chad," Janine advised, nudging Jill to stand up. "It's a special night for her."

"No problem, Janine." He raised his hands and finger-combed Jill's hair, lifting the sides and allowing them to fall back down onto her shoulders. "A bit of shaping; a perm would be nice."

"Perm?" Jill squeaked, remembering the Tonis her mother used to give her and how she'd end up looking like Shirley Temple.

"No problem, sweetheart. When I finish, you will look gorgeous." Chad snaked an arm around Jill's waist and led her to the back. She turned around, throwing Janine a beseeching look, which her friend cheerfully ignored.

"I'll be back later." Janine left Jill to her fate. "I told you a perm was what you needed."

Jill wasn't sure what to expect in this salon, where the loud music threatened to give her a headache and looking at some of the crazily dressed hairdressers left her feeling like someone thrust in the midst of aliens.

"You're a real foxy lady, Jill." A few hours later Chad used a pick to heighten the hair along her crown. "Is there anyone special in your life?"

Jill glanced up, gauging him to be no older than

twenty-five. She searched his face for signs of teasing but couldn't find any. He was serious!

"Well, ah, there is someone," she managed to stammer out. At the same time she wondered how much it would take for her to be enticed by this bewitching man's offer. It was obvious he wanted to take her out.

"Well, if you change your mind, call me . . . anytime." Chad's smile oozed with sensuality, echoing his invitation.

Jill still couldn't believe her ears. She imagined this sexy guy pursuing some young thing in a leather miniskirt and fishnet hose. Any man who wore a V-neck sweater and extremely tight white jeans that left nothing to the imagination couldn't want a woman who was just turning thirty. She reached for the glass of champagne Chad had given her earlier.

"My, it's warm in here," she said weakly, sipping the bubbly liquid.

Chad wore a knowing smile when he whisked the cape from Jill's shoulders a moment later. He obviously assumed he had another conquest in this classy lady.

"I love it!" Janine squealed, fingering the loose waves that framed Jill's face. "Wear your drop-dead black dress tonight. Greg deserves the full treatment."

An hour later Janine was in the midst of applying base makeup to Jill's face when Jill told her about Chad's invitation.

"Really?" Janine chuckled. "Well, you have to admit that he is some kind of hunk. Too bad he never propositioned me. I'd probably take him up on it." She dipped a fat, soft-bristled brush into translucent loose powder, flicked the brush over her palm, then dusted Jill's face. Blusher followed next; then a smoky blue-gray shadow and coordinating kohl pencil deepened the blue of Jill's eyes.

"You know, maybe thirty isn't so bad after all," Jill meditated, studying her reflection in the mirror. "After all, they say that's the beginning of a woman's sexual peak."

"So take full advantage of it," Janine advised, rummaging through Jill's closet. "Ah, here it is!" She pulled out a black strapless dress and held it up. "Where are your black pumps?"

"The Charles Jourdan box." Jill was still busy looking at herself in the mirror. She looked so different . . . sexy. The idea excited her.

She still felt that way as she adjusted the three hooks that were all that held the dress together. As she walked, the side fold parted to reveal slender thighs encased in sheer black stockings. Her black pumps showed off shapely ankles. She applied a deep rose lipstick and a shimmery lip gloss and wore diamond and sapphire earrings as her only jewelry.

"Thank you, Janine." She hugged her friend.

"I survived my thirtieth birthday six months ago, so I knew you'd make it." Janine smiled. She glanced at the clock. "I'd better go. Have a great time." She tipped her head to one side and smiled in that mysterious way Jill recognized only too well. "In fact, I'm sure you'll have a *wonderful* time."

"I don't want to hear it," Jill protested. "In fact, why don't you run along and find your future husband?"

"I don't need to. He'll come to me. Call me tomorrow and tell me all about your evening."

Jill didn't have much time to herself before Greg

tapped on her door and entered. He froze, taking in her appearance from head to toe before blurting out, "What did you do to your hair, put your finger in a light socket?"

CHAPTER SIX

Jill was stunned by Greg's candid statement. "This happens to be very chic, and *I* like it." She enunciated each word carefully. That man could deflate her ego with the fewest words!

Greg was astute enough to back off before Jill tore his head off. He almost asked how she managed to keep her dress up, but decided not to push his luck. That was when he held out a gift-wrapped box. "Happy birthday. I know you didn't want to celebrate it, but I figured you wouldn't turn down a gift."

Jill eyed the elaborately wrapped square box with suspicion. "Are snakes going to pop out of it, like last year's gift?"

"No, that was only appropriate for a twenty-ninth birthday." He grinned.

Jill took the small box from him and carefully undid the wrapping. What she didn't expect was a beautiful gold pendant with a fire opal set in the center of the intricate design. "Oh, Greg!" she breathed, fingering the swirls of gold. She looked up, unable to understand why she felt like crying. "It's beautiful." She stepped forward to give him a thank-you kiss, but when their lips met it didn't feel as casual as it had the other times they exchanged light, friendly kisses. Their mouths began to soften and move to find just the right spot instead of dispensing with a light peck at the lips.

Greg's fingertips rested lightly on Jill's hip, and he found himself fighting the urge to pull her into his arms and kiss her thoroughly. He felt a sense of need during the short exchange—a need for much more.

Jill stepped back quickly, searching Greg's face for the same questions plaguing her; she wasn't disappointed. He was just as surprised as she.

"We'd better go," Greg said hoarsely, breaking the thick silence between them.

Jill nodded, allowing him to assist her with her coat. They walked down the stairs, their shoulders brushing along the way. Jill felt as if she was going out on a date, not just going out with a good friend; the idea was somewhat unnerving. Still, she had wondered what he would be like in that category, so why shouldn't she just relax and enjoy it?

Dinner passed in a haze for Jill. They ate at her favorite restaurant, and during those hours they found themselves talking more openly than they had before and learning new things about each other. Jill discovered that Greg had suffered a good spanking at the age of five for cutting his younger sister's hair in a crew cut. She confessed to the time she and her sister had decided to paint a picture on the bathroom wall using the oil paints from a paint-by-number kit they had received for Christmas. They hadn't been allowed to play with their friends for a month. And with each reminiscence, another followed.

Dessert was a succulent chocolate soufflé with brandy afterward.

"Greg," Jill said as she drew her scarlet-tipped

103

nail across the white linen tablecloth, "thank you so much for a lovely evening."

"It isn't over yet, beautiful," he informed her, slipping a charge card inside the leather folder that held the bill. "Think you're up to some dancing?"

Her eyes sparkled with anticipation. "Try me!"

It wasn't long before Greg regretted his decision to give Jill a wild night on the town. When they entered the private club he belonged to, he soon discovered that he wasn't the only man interested in the way Jill's dress parted all the way up to her thigh when she walked. Funny, it had never bothered him before when men admired the woman he was with, because it heightened his ego. But this time he wanted to slip Jill's coat back on her and hustle her out the door. He glared at one man who appeared more than interested in Jill's legs.

"Over here," Greg muttered in her ear, steering her to a table in a dimly lit corner.

"Wait, there's one near the dance floor." She pulled on his hand.

He cursed under his breath as they wove their way between the crowded tables. It took all his concentration to reply to several scattered greetings from friends. He didn't bother looking around because he was too busy watching the enticing sway of Jill's hips as she walked in front of him.

Greg ordered champagne from the waitress before allowing Jill to pull him out on the dance floor. She threw her arms over her head, wiggled her hips and moved seductively with the music. Greg had no choice but to move along with her. The next song was slow and sensual, prompting him to step forward and take Jill into his arms.

"This is a first for us," he commented, keeping

104

his hands on her hips so that her arms wound around his neck.

Jill tipped her head back, her lashes half covering her vividly colored eyes. She could feel the heated strength of his chest against her breasts and found the sensation exciting. For one brief second a startling thought flew through her mind. *I could fall in love with this man!* "Oh?"

"Sure." His dark mood rapidly evaporated under her spell, not to mention the warm scent of her perfume drifting up from her skin. He felt tempted to lean down and kiss the bare slope of her shoulder and find out if she tasted as good as she looked and smelled. "Do you realize in all the time we've known each other we've never danced together before?"

"What do you mean we've never danced together? Of course we have. Don't you remember my New Year's Eve party?" she reminded him. "There was dancing then."

Greg shook his head. "We were otherwise occupied."

Jill sobered. Funny, she assumed there wasn't anything she and Greg had not done. Well, there was *one* thing. The champagne must be affecting her wits for her to think so easily along those lines. She freely admitted that she thought of Greg as a sexy man, but for the sake of their working relationship, she vowed to try to keep it to herself.

It was a birthday celebration to end all celebrations. It didn't take them long to drain the bottle of champagne. Hours later the tipsy pair left the club and poured themselves into a taxi.

"Come up for a drink," Jill invited, her words slower than usual.

"Think you can handle more?" Greg asked, paying the driver and following her up the stairs to her apartment.

"Shue—sho—sure." She laughingly wondered why one simple word could be so difficult to say. Inside her apartment, she stepped out of her high heels and sashayed into the kitchen, humming one of the songs they had danced to that evening. "Think we should stick with champagne?"

"Safer." Greg half collapsed on her couch before realizing he still had his topcoat on. After a few major contortions he finally discarded it, not caring that it fell to the floor.

"Ta-da!" Jill caroled, dancing into the room holding a bottle and two fluted glasses aloft. With a flourish she presented the foil-tipped bottle to Greg.

He screwed his face up in a comic expression of distaste when he studied the label. "This is pink champagne."

Jill retrieved the bottle, holding it up so she could read the label. "Yep, it's pink all right," she agreed with the solemnity of one who is quite drunk. "Peter—you 'member him? He brought it to the party. We just didn't drink it."

"Real men don't drink pink champagne," Greg intoned, looking up at her with bleary eyes.

Giggling, Jill dropped down onto the couch next to him. "Oh, Greg, that's awful. Promise you won't write a book with that title." She found the last word difficult to pronounce.

Greg shook his head. "Nope, never sell." It took him a few moments to release the cork and pour the bubbling liquid into the two glasses. "To an old lady's thirtieth birthday," he toasted, but missed clinking Jill's glass. She laughed as if it were the funniest trick she had ever seen.

106

Jill sipped her champagne and held her glass up. "To the even older man who can't toast worth a damn." She polished off her drink and poured more into her glass.

"To the woman with the electric hair."

"To the man who most resembles Hairy Harry."

The level of the bottle quickly lowered as toasts of every subject imaginable were made.

"To our fifth anniversary of working together," Greg announced.

"That's not for three more months," Jill objected. "I wish you'd stop swaying." She didn't realize she was moving in the opposite direction.

Greg squinted, concentrating on pulling the two hazy Jills into one clear one. "To Hairy Harry—may his adventures continue selling."

"You said it." Jill's hiccup and giggle escaped at the same time.

He smiled, even though it looked a bit lopsided. "To the most beautiful woman I've ever known."

Jill pouted. "How about the entire world?"

"Don't press your luck."

The alcohol-induced euphoria didn't last long. Jill curled up on the couch, unaware that the folds of her dress had fallen away to the top of her thighs. She stared at Greg with her lower lip wobbling and her eyes liquid with tears.

"Greg, I'm getting old," she whispered in a shaky voice. "I've found some gray hairs, and I know there are wrinkles around my eyes. Oh, they may be small now, but they'll get bigger; I just know it. Pretty soon I'll have to have a face-lift or go to Europe for those placenta treatments."

If Greg had been sober he would have laughed and teased Jill out of her fears. But he was beginning to feel just as low. He pulled her into his arms

107

and settled her on his lap, cuddling her the way he would a small child.

"Hey, it's not so bad," he soothed, rubbing her back. "I bet you'll be a great-looking old lady. Who knows, you could turn out to be a matriarch known for her ageless beauty."

"Sure," she said with a sniff, rubbing her nose with the back of her hand. "I'll be there wearing support hose, oxfords and tweeds."

"You forgot your girdle," he said.

Jill would have punched him in the stomach, but she missed and her hand connected with the couch arm next to Greg instead. "Where's the comfort you're supposed to show me?" she demanded.

"Comfort." He wrapped his arms closer around her. At that moment their faces almost collided. He might have been drunk, but he certainly wasn't stupid. He dipped his face down further and kissed her lightly on the lips, paused, looked down into her eyes and moved his lips over hers again. This time the pressure increased with alarming pleasure.

Jill linked her arms around his neck and relaxed to enjoy the varied movements of their lips. "Where did you learn to kiss so well?" she asked, opening her eyes wide so she could see clearly.

"Raquel Welch."

She shook her head. "I'm not that drunk."

Greg brushed his mouth over Jill's again. "Liz Barnhart," he murmured, again warming her mouth with his. "I was a tender fourteen and she was a very experienced woman of sixteen. She deserved a Ph.D. in oscillation."

"Mmm, and you made straight A's in the course." She brought his face down to hers for more.

Their kisses became light, almost teasing, and Jill's arms remained around Greg's neck as his hands rotated against the base of her spine. Anyone walking in would have thought two teenagers were indulging in a heavy necking session. Soon their mouths parted and Greg's tongue bathed Jill's lower lip before delving inside to search out her moist sweetness.

"Kiss me," he whispered.

She complied without hesitation, eager to taste him again. She also felt the slight roughness of his skin below the smooth lip glistening from her moist touch. Unable to stop at that, Jill's tongue followed the curved line of his upper lip and slipped inside. A soft, throaty moan left his throat at her daring. His arms tightened around her hips and one hand moved upward to bury itself in the silky curls spilling down over her nape.

"Do you realize how well you fit in my arms?" His husky voice revealed the arousal his body had already shown her.

"Pink champagne certainly tastes better on you," she murmured, tracing his ear with her fingertips.

"I heartily agree." He nuzzled the soft and very vulnerable spot of her throat. "But I like this much better. And this." He found another enticing area along her shoulder. "And especially this." He kissed the top of her breast, which was barely hidden by the black silk.

Jill drew in a sharp breath at the fire racing through her veins. With Greg's cheek resting against her breast, she knew he would feel her nipple pucker in reaction to his touch. She wondered what it would feel like to have his mouth take possession of the aching bud. She ran her fingers over his face as she inclined her head to nip his earlobe and down to slant her parted lips over his.

"Oh, yes, Liz Barnhart taught you very well," she

whispered in a voice breathy from the passion flowing between them. Jill could feel the heat building up in the middle of her body and flowering outward, seeking surcease. She wiggled her fingers between the buttons of his shirt to feel the heat of his skin.

Greg lay back on the couch with Jill over him. "You've got sexy legs, Jill," he murmured, edging one hand under the hem of her dress and up her thigh. "I always like summertime because you wear those cute shorts that outline your curvy tush."

"This does not sound like a man who writes about a gorilla attending preschool," Jill gurgled.

He pressed his hand against her buttocks until her hips were cradled against his. His hands moved along Jill's sides, skimmed over her breasts and shoulders, then tunneled through her hair, his palms warming her ears. She was powerless when his mouth ground ruthlessly against hers. They shared each other's breath as their tongues met, playing seductively. It wasn't long before both were breathing harshly. Jill's eyes drifted shut so she could allow the beauty of Greg's touch to wash over her. She couldn't remember any man taking her to these heights just by kissing her. As far as she was concerned, Greg was more than welcome to carry her into the bedroom and finish this wonderful experience.

Easily reading her thoughts, he sat up, keeping his arms around her as if he was loath to give her up. "This isn't the time, Jill." His voice was gritty with passion. "We've both had too much to drink, and while I want very badly to make love to you, I also want us cold sober so there won't be any repercussions the next morning." He still couldn't resist running his palm over her shoulder. That same palm itched to caress her breast, but he knew if he touched her further it would be all over before it could truly begin. He glanced away, unable to look at her glistening and swollen lips, knowing he was the one responsible.

"Are you sure you want to do this?" Jill asked, using her forefinger to trace an imaginary line along his jaw. She suddenly felt powerful in her femininity. "Or should I say, not do this?"

Greg looked up at the ceiling, laughing out his frustration. "Believe me, babe, the last thing I want to do is leave, but it's for the best." He set her upright on the couch, stood and reached for his coat.

Jill couldn't believe what she was hearing. "You—you're just going to leave?" She was incredulous, not to mention disappointed. "You're joking, aren't you?"

He shook his head, a faint smile touching his lips. "Jill, I only wish this were a joke, but this isn't the time for us." He leaned over, kissed her on the forehead and walked to the door. "Happy birthday," he said as he left.

Jill leaned over to extract a cigarette from the box on the coffee table and picked up her lighter. She curled up against the couch arm and lit up, pulling the smoke into her lungs and slowly blowing it out. It was just what she needed to calm her quivering nerve endings; at least it was a poor imitation. She finally got up and went into the bedroom, not bothering to clean up the empty champagne bottle and two glasses, which was an excellent barometer of her jumbled emotions. Her clothes were dropped carelessly onto the carpet and she slid into bed without bothering with a nightgown.

111

The strident whine of a vacuum cleaner sliced through Jill's tender brain like a hot knife. She shot up in bed, holding the sheet up to her chin.

"Oh, please, Mrs. Hathaway," she moaned. "Not now."

The older woman appeared in the doorway. "About time you woke up." She eyed the strewn clothes with distaste.

Jill covered her eyes with the heels of her hands in the hope of blocking out the white dots dancing a polka before her. "What time is it?"

"Two o'clock in the afternoon. A late hour even for you." The housekeeper glanced toward the open bathroom door as if expecting a man to appear. "I still have to clean up in here," she announced with a sour purse of the lips. She had no sympathy for hangovers.

"Okay." Her head was killing her from the inside!

"I'll be leaving soon," the older woman reminded her.

"Fine." Jill wondered if her face was still in one piece or if it had scattered all over the bed.

"Then I guess I'll finish the living room," Mrs. Hathaway decided, moving away and slamming the bedroom door behind her.

"Ooh," Jill moaned as the loud sound pierced her eardrums. She climbed out of bed, only to stagger into the bathroom for a reviving shower.

She stood under the streaming jets of hot water, allowing the steam to clear her head for more rational thoughts. They soon came, fast and furious.

Had she really kissed Greg back last night? Had they really almost made love? Had she really felt more aroused than she had in a long time? Last but not least, had an equally aroused Greg left her to sleep alone? She groaned at the memories crowding her bruised brain. She didn't know whether to feel relieved or upset that Greg had left her alone.

Jill allowed her hair to dry on its own and only bothered with a light coating of moisturizer on her face. She dressed in a bright turquoise warmup suit with a band of bright yellow crossing the front and back. While the bright color was meant to lift her spirits, it certainly didn't flatter her pale complexion. She put on a pair of glasses with tinted lenses to shield her sensitive eyes and left the apartment.

"'Bout time some people decided to join the living," Mrs. Hathaway muttered, steering the vacuum cleaner into the bedroom.

Greg was downstairs pretending to work and performing a horrible job of it. A bottle of aspirin and a pitcher of orange juice stood near his elbow. While trying to work at the computer terminal, he had soon discovered that the amber letters on the monitor made his headache worse, so he sat at his desk, writing out ideas for new books.

"This is all your fault." Jill's croak sounded from behind him.

Greg turned his head very carefully, positive it would splinter into a million pieces if he moved too quickly. "You're talking too loud." He closed his eyes. "Did you have to wear such a bright color? It's enough to blind a man," he grumbled, turning back.

"I figured I'd look more alive in this than if I wore black." She picked up the glass of orange juice sitting near his elbow and sipped the tart liquid to cool her cotton-filled throat.

"Why are you wearing glasses when you don't need them?" he demanded.

"For effect," she replied sardonically. "All serious writers wear glasses."

"You haven't been serious since day one," Greg retorted.

"Ha, ha, very funny." Jill poured more juice into the glass and drank deeply.

"Get your own glass." He snatched it out of her hand. It wasn't that he resented her drinking out of his glass. They had certainly shared drinking glasses many times in the past. But not when *he* wanted to be the one to moisten her lips. Greg couldn't help wondering if they would have felt better this morning if they had given in to their baser instincts and made love all night. He certainly couldn't be feeling any worse than he already was! He might have been drunk when he went to bed hours before, but it hadn't dimmed the ache in his body. Now the pale-faced embodiment of his desires sat before him, and even with red-rimmed eyes, a pasty complexion and shaky hands, she still looked beautiful to his bloodshot eyes.

Jill's thoughts were along the same lines as Greg's. She had always seen him as a good-looking and desirable man, but even more erotic doors were opening in her mind. He was one of her best friends and someone she could talk to about any subject, but she suddenly thought of him as more than just someone to talk to. She had always believed there was a distinct purpose in everything that happened to a person. Were her and Greg's previous lovers merely a prelude to what they would eventually share with each other? The thought both frightened and fascinated her. It was just as well she didn't realize that his thoughts were traveling along the same lines.

"It was probably the pink champagne that did it," Greg mumbled.

Jill discovered smiling didn't hurt her face any longer. "Did what?"

"Left us feeling like hell."

"Peter never did have good taste in wine," she murmured. "Do you feel guilty about last night?" She couldn't resist asking.

"No," he answered without hesitation.

She reached for the glass of orange juice. "Neither do I." Jill slid her glasses up on top of her head. "I think Mrs. Hathaway is convinced I participated in an orgy last night." She discovered she was feeling more like her normal self.

"Knowing that sour-faced old witch, she probably thinks I make love to you on your desk every day." Greg bit his lip, unable to believe he had actually spoken out loud one of his more erotic fantasies.

Jill didn't have much difficulty visualizing such a dream. "Have you worked on the book any more?" She knew she had to return to reality before she said or did something ridiculous.

Greg sensed her unease and answered in a careless tone, "My brain wasn't ready for that, so I've just been fooling around with new ideas."

"Oh, what have you come up with?"

The rest of the afternoon passed under a thick cloud of sexual tension. Neither one of them could work without being aware of each movement of the other. Jill covertly watched Greg's thigh muscles flex when he shifted position in his chair. He noticed the rise and fall of her breasts under her top and remembered how they felt to his touch. He wanted to recreate that feeling again. After a couple of hours they still hadn't been able to accomplish any true work.

"We might as well quit for the day," Greg announced, throwing his pen down. He stretched his arms over his head to relieve the ache in his shoulders. "Want to go out for some dinner?"

"As long as we don't order champagne," Jill replied. "My head won't be able to handle another day like today."

"We could go to the Fargo Station," he suggested.

She nodded. "Give me time to change my clothes." She raised herself out of her chair. "I can be downstairs in about an hour."

Greg nodded. "Fine with me. I should have the rest of the fuzz out of my head by then."

Jill took another shower, applied a light touch of makeup, and dressed in designer jeans, low-heeled boots and an argyle sweater with blocks of jade, cobalt and plum against a black background. For an added touch she wore her new pendant. Greg had dressed just as casually in jeans and a steel blue sweater.

The Fargo Station was one of their favorite eating places. With an interior resembling a saloon out of a Western film, it also boasted old-fashioned photographs of mining camps and Wanted posters of famous and not-so-famous outlaws on the walls. Jill and Greg were greeted by a hostess dressed like a schoolmarm, who led them to the Black Bart room.

"Y'all want a beer or cocktail before you order?" she asked in her sugary Alabama drawl.

Jill resisted the urge to groan loudly. "Just club soda," she requested, pulling out her cigarettes and lighter.

Greg asked for a draft beer.

Jill studied the menu, which consisted of various cuts of steak, prime rib and wild game when available.

"Venison sounds good," Greg remarked, looking up from his menu.

Jill's head snapped up, her eyes wide saucers. "Venison?" Her voice rose. "You would eat Bambi?"

"You're overreacting, Jill," he protested in a harsh whisper. "Besides, Bambi was a fawn."

"Who grew up," she argued.

He looked at her as if he couldn't believe what he was hearing. When had she become so unreasonable? This had never happened before when they had eaten here. "All right, if it's going to bother you so much, I'll order rabbit stew instead."

"Thumper was a rabbit," she pointed out.

"No more Disney movies for you." Greg shook his head, astonished that someone could be so matter-of-fact one moment and completely emotional the next. This woman was turning him inside out! He didn't care to realize that the reason for their minor disagreements was due to the events of the previous night.

"I'm going to have the steak, ladies' cut," Jill announced.

"Steak comes from a cow," Greg informed her with a perfectly straight face. "Makes me think of Susie, my calf."

Jill flashed a brief smile at the waitress when she set the glass of club soda in front of her. After they ordered, she eyed Greg suspiciously. "Gregory Mark Richmond, you grew up in Santa Barbara where your father still owns a prosperous restaurant and your mother runs a successful real estate agency. The 'ranch' house you lived in had two dogs, a cat and an aquarium filled with tropical fish. As far as I know, you've never even been within petting distance of a calf."

"I certainly did own a calf." He looked affronted at her accusation. "Susie was part of my farm animal play set."

Jill choked on her drink before glaring at Greg with all her might. "Talk about low. You've pulled some dirty tricks on me before, but this is the worst."

Greg settled back in the captain's chair, his hands clasped, the fingers touching to form a steeple. "You're a strange mixture, Jill," he mused. "Has any man ever learned the true you?"

"Isn't it better to be a lady of mystery?" she quipped with a coy lift of her shoulders.

He didn't smile as he continued watching her. "Not you; at least not to everyone."

"Meaning you."

"Meaning me."

Jill accepted her steak, baked potato and baked beans. A basket of warm Indian fry bread and sourdough bread was deposited on the table. She concentrated on cutting the meat into tiny pieces, then adding butter to her potato; she would do anything rather than look at Greg. She took a bite of each and added a slice of bread to her plate. Sensing his gaze on her, she finally looked up to find him watching her in a disconcerting way.

"You know all about me, Greg," she argued softly. "In fact, you probably know almost as much as Janine does."

"Do I?" he countered just as softly, also cutting his meat. He caught the waitress's eye and requested another beer and asked Jill if she'd care for something else to drink. She asked for an iced tea.

"Greg, what exactly are you getting at?" she asked abruptly.

He chuckled. "That's my girl, cut straight to the

heart of the matter. We're very much alike, you know."

"Perhaps in some ways." Jill surprised Greg by agreeing calmly. "Although your lovers certainly outnumber mine." Now why did she have to say that? And why did the thought bother her so much?

He gripped his fork tightly. "I didn't realize we were keeping score," he spit out.

"I don't want to fight with you, Greg." She sighed, for once not allowing her temper to take over.

He breathed deeply, finally acknowledging the same.

"Okay, killer, let's eat as if there's no tomorrow, then go over to visit Tank," Jill recommended brightly, reaching across the table to take his hand.

He smiled and lifted her hand, pressing a kiss in her palm, then curling her fingers inward to hold his kiss. "Sounds fine to me."

Greg and Jill stayed at Mahoney's until closing time nursing one drink each. It was as if they were afraid drinking too much would bring on a repeat of the previous night's episode, and they both knew they weren't ready for that.

CHAPTER SEVEN

For the next few days Jill and Greg worked in their own offices, but even that small separation didn't lessen their heightened awareness of each other.

There were times Greg would swear he smelled Jill's perfume drifting through the air.

Jill recognized every tune Greg hummed to himself as the songs they had danced to on her birthday.

In other words, they were slowly but steadily getting on each other's nerves.

"Do you think you could lay off wearing clothing that doesn't glow in the dark for a while?" Greg demanded one morning when Jill arrived downstairs wearing a hot pink jumpsuit that showed off every curve and a reasonable amount of cleavage.

Her reply was short and to the point. "Would you mind not using your desk as a set of drums? Who do you think you are, Gene Krupa?"

"Gene Krupa, huh? You're certainly older than thirty if you know about him," he said with a sneer.

"It's amazing what the late night shows can teach you. You should try it sometime," she advised kindly. "You might learn something."

"Sure, then I'd be just as smart as you. I'd learn who Superman really is, and what good ole Boris and Bela are doing in those movies, not to mention your favorite gory films on cable. That kind of education I can do without, thank you," he jeered.

Jill's eyes narrowed to deep blue slits. The battle was on, and she was ready to fight.

"It's certainly meatier than watching your English drawing room comedies."

"And you think that planets eating people, rocks that are really aliens and the lizard who ate downtown New Orleans are educational?" Greg fought back. "You wouldn't know culture if it walked up to you and introduced itself."

"Some of those movies you're maligning happen to be classics," she argued hotly, standing in front of him with her hands braced on her hips. Her entire body quivered with relish at the idea of an all-out battle. It was just what she needed.

"To some people they may be classics, but that's because you don't have to worry about testing your brain power!" he shouted, waving his hands about in an arc.

"That is really low, Greg," Jill countered, a brief smile on her lips. "I certainly didn't insult your mediocre intelligence." She picked her cigarette up from the ashtray and puffed on it, knowing she was making matters worse. It was probably a childish gesture, but the only one she could think of at the moment.

Greg's mouth tightened in annoyance. For one moment he thought about strangling her. The trouble was, if he put his hands on her he feared his dark mood would rapidly change into something more powerful.

The two combatants stood glaring at each other in the middle of the room. Then the hard set of Greg's jaw relaxed just a bit. "You know the reason we're acting like this, don't you?"

"I might," she said, cautious of what he might be leading up to.

His gaze swept over her rigid figure. "Your place or mine?" he quipped, his eyes returning to stare at her face.

Jill's expression didn't reveal her inner feelings. She thought this particular scene should be in a movie, not played out in the midst of an office when bedrooms were so easily accessible to them.

"We're both acting like a couple of crazy monkeys at the zoo," she said softly, lowering her stiff shoulders a fraction.

"Even monkeys have those holes in the corner leading to a private area." Greg found himself wanting to pick Jill up and carry her upstairs. "Sexual frustration can turn into anger and temper tantrums. It appears we qualify on both. Jill, we need to do something about it."

She arched an eyebrow, looking much too smug for his peace of mind. If he had been able to see into her brain he would have discovered that she agreed wholeheartedly. "I wouldn't know about such things."

"Damnit, Jill!" Greg exploded, moving away from the spot he had previously been frozen to. "This is not some little feature story in the morning paper for you to make asinine jokes over." He crossed the room in two steps until he stood directly in front of her. If he leaned down a few more inches their noses would touch.

"I want you, Jill," he said bluntly, gripping her shoulders. "And it's only too apparent that you feel the same." His gaze raked over her, noting the signs of her arousal—her peaked nipples through the thin material, her thrusting breasts asking for his touch and her rapid breathing.

For the first time Jill couldn't think of a come-back. She could only look up at him and wonder why this hadn't happened before. How had they managed to remain apart so long?

Impatient with Jill's hesitation, Greg jerked her toward him and fastened his mouth on hers in one smooth motion.

Jill was past vacillating. She curled her arms around his neck and moved in even closer. Their mouths met hungrily as if they couldn't get enough of each other. His lips moved upward to caress each eye and sweep across her forehead.

"I guess these crazy curls aren't so bad after all." His breath warmed her skin. "They just show off new places for me to kiss." He flicked his tongue under one such curl. He took a deep breath, but it wasn't enough to calm his racing blood. "Come on," he said harshly, unsure if his voice would even hold for those few words.

Jill wasn't about to argue when Greg led her up-stairs to his apartment. Inside, she had to watch her step so she wouldn't trip over the articles of cloth-ing scattered on the living room carpet as she was pulled into the bedroom. Jill only had a moment to notice a damp towel lying across the bathroom doorway, the cream and rust abstract print quilt that had been pushed to the floor and the top sheet draped over it. An open book sat on the pillow and a faint drift of Greg's aftershave still lingered in the air, along with another smell coming from the kitchen area; Greg must have burned his breakfast.

Clothing had never been discarded so quickly. The book suddenly flew across the room, thanks to Greg. He adjusted the miniblinds so only a mini-mum of light slid across the bed. He returned to Jill, gathering her in his arms and pressing hot kisses across her face. By shifting his weight, they fell across the bed in delicious abandon, prepared for what would happen.

And happen it did. Greg nuzzled Jill's breasts, the flat plane of her stomach, and the tops of her thighs. He learned the soft skin under her arms, discovered the floral scent of her perfume along her throat and behind her ears and learned what her eyelashes felt like against his skin.

Jill explored the silky dark hair on Greg's chest, found out he was ticklish along his right side and watched his nipples pucker under the loving touch of her tongue.

When Greg moved over Jill, entering her in one thrust, she looked up and saw what looked like a footprint on the ceiling. A footprint? That was something she didn't care to pursue any further. What was wrong? Why weren't they flying into another galaxy, as they had on her birthday?

Greg realized how easily Jill's pelvis cradled his body, but while their loving should have been wonderful, something was missing. Where was the wonder of their joining, the ecstasy, the pleasure?

Five minutes later it was over. Jill and Greg lay on the bed, each taking up a separate half, staring up at the ceiling.

"Isn't this the part where we smoke our cigarettes and gaze upward?" Jill finally spoke the words that had plagued them both.

Greg turned his head, wondering where the magic had gone. "Maybe the timing was wrong."

She shot him a look filled with pity. "And you accuse me of being the dreamer," she chided him, raising herself up on one elbow. With her tangled hair hanging to her shoulders and ribbons of faint sunlight crossing her body, she presented an alluring picture. "Greg, we made a mistake in going to bed together, and we could have ruined our friendship because of this. We'd better quit while we're ahead."

He strongly disagreed. "What we just shared is another part of friendship."

Jill sat up in bed, stretching her arms high over her head. With her eyes closed, she didn't see Greg's intent gaze on her uplifted breasts peeking above the sheet covering her to the waist.

What happened? the little man in his brain insisted on knowing. You had the most authentic woman of a lifetime in your bed and you blew it! You'd better do something about it fast!

I rushed it, he apologized to his conscience. I didn't see beyond my own desires, and we should have taken it slower. The trouble is, I don't know if I could have lasted much longer. He flipped the sheet over him and watched Jill slip out of bed and pull on a pair of cream-colored bikini pants and pull her jumpsuit up. When she finished dressing, she sat on the edge of the bed, one arm braced near his hip.

"Don't go all masculine ego on me, Greg," she warned lightly. "Hey, we tried something and it didn't work. No sweat."

"No sweat? Thanks for acting so damned understanding about it." His voice grated, stung by her careless words.

Jill's smile didn't waver. "At least we're still friends."

She could have been his mother reassuring him that while he might hate his best friend today, everything would be all right tomorrow. He was beginning to think that it might not be too difficult to dislike her.

"If you don't mind, I'd like to take a shower," he said gruffly, watching her with such cold eyes they seemed to freeze her all the way to her spine.

"You'll understand what I mean when you think it over," she assured him, standing up. "I'll see you tomorrow."

Greg remained in bed until he heard the front door quietly close, then he picked up his pillow and threw it against the wall.

He knew only too well that if the situation had been different, Jill would still be in bed with him and they would be exploring paradise again. He didn't know why everything had gone wrong. It could have been for any number of reasons. Who knows, maybe thier biorhythms were off or their astrological signs were in the wrong house or their auras didn't match or—but he wasn't going to give up. He couldn't believe that what they had shared the night of Jill's birthday had only been a fluke. He knew they were basically meant for each other. All he had to do was convince Jill of that.

Jill entered her own apartment and walked into the kitchen. She retrieved a bowl from a cabinet and a spoon and knife from a drawer before taking a covered cake pan from the pantry. A large square of brownie was carefully placed in the bowl, followed by three large scoops of French vanilla ice cream with hot fudge sauce poured over that.

"Might as well go all the way," she murmured. Taking a can of whipped cream out of the refrigerator, she topped the hot fudge with the fluffy white confection and added chopped nuts. Jill set the bowl on the table and sat down to eat every last calorie-filled bite. After her snack she wandered into the bedroom and stripped off her clothes. She entered the bathroom and turned on the shower, waiting a few moments before stepping under the steaming water. She soaped her body automatically and wasn't sure if the droplets of water covering her cheeks were tears or not.

Jill was in the midst of her second hot fudge brownie sundae when the downstairs buzzer intruded.

"Yes?" She spoke into the small intercom, not really caring to see anyone.

"Let me in." Janine's voice sounded fuzzy through the speaker.

Jill pressed the button to release the outside door before returning to the couch and her food. It didn't take Janine long to climb the stairs.

"Um, looks good." She looked down at the bowl. "Is there enough for one more?"

"Plenty." Jill waved her hand toward the kitchen. "Help yourself. No offense, but what are you doing here?" She made sure she had an equal portion of brownie, ice cream, fudge and whipped cream on her spoon before lifting it to her lips.

Janine tapped her lightly on the head. "I knew you would need me." She disappeared into the kitchen.

"I don't want to hear it, Janine!" Jill shouted, licking a speck of hot fudge off the back of her spoon. "In fact, I'm getting very tired of your little flashes of insight."

"I told you not to let your first impressions disappoint you. Actually, I guess it would be more second impressions than first." Janine waltzed out of the kitchen carrying a bowl filled with the same rich snack. She dropped into a chair and eyed Jill with that discerning gaze of hers, seeing more than she would let on. "Besides, all I'd have to do is look at the evidence, namely the brownies. At this rate you'll be three hundred pounds by midnight." She dipped her spoon into the rich brown and white treat. "Is this that milk chocolate hot fudge from that new gourmet shop?"

Jill nodded glumly, eating absently. As if coming out of a daze, she turned to Janine, seeing her for the very first time. "If I ask you never to warn or advise me about the future again, will you heed my wish?"

"Of course." She didn't appear surprised by the request, but looking down at her dish, couldn't resist asking, "You did remember to refill your prescription last month, didn't you?"

Jill's face first registered horror, then relief overshadowed it, followed by exasperation at her friend. "I hope that man you intend to marry is cross-eyed."

"He's not," Janine murmured with just a hint of a smile crossing her lips.

"What?" Jill set her bowl on the coffee table and turned in her seat. "Are you telling me that you've already met him?"

"Kenneth Randolph Salisbury the third." The dreamy expression in Janine's eyes said it all. "He is so-o-o sexy."

Jill shook her head in disbelief. "He sounds as if he belongs to one of the city's first families."

Janine shook her head. "He owns an inn outside Sacramento. He's here to meet with a contractor about building several bungalows on the property. Would you believe he saw me at the restaurant that day and kept returning there in the hope of seeing me again?" Jill couldn't remember ever seeing Janine looking so excited.

"And naturally you've been eating lunch there every day," Jill commented, at that moment hating anyone who was happy while she felt as if she had joined the dregs of the earth.

Janine took another bite of her treat before setting the bowl down. Dressed in a ruby velour top and jeans, with her dark hair piled on top of her head in loose curls, she resembled an exotic jewel. "Although you'll undoubtedly leave out the juicy parts, I'd like to hear what happened between you and Greg." She wasn't avid for gossip, only concerned for her friend.

Jill tucked her amethyst terry robe under her bare feet when she curled them up under her. "You clash horribly with that chair," she mused, hoping that if she changed the subject, Janine would get the idea she didn't want to talk about Greg. One look at her serene yet stubborn face told her differently. She sighed. "Okay, let's just say we're better off friends than lovers." She was determined not to say any more.

Janine figured out the rest of the story without any problem. "No fireworks, no violins?"

"Not one tiny flute." Jill laughed harshly. "And yet that man kisses as if there's only one woman for him and you're it."

"You are." Janine ignored Jill's warning glare. "And here I tried to entice him and lost out."

Jill stared at Janine as if the woman sitting nearby were a perfect stranger instead of someone she had known for years. "You made a pass at Greg?" she squeaked, tamping down the hot streak of jealousy streaking through her. "When?"

"Tyler's barbecue last summer," Janine replied a bit too serenely. "If you remember, Greg and Barbara had just broken up."

"Yes." Jill spoke softly, almost to herself. She remembered the barbecue at a friend's house only too well. She had gone with Cal, and Greg went alone. Now that she thought about it, she did remember Janine and Greg spending a great deal of time together. In fact, Greg had taken Janine home. "I'm surprised you never told me about it before now," she said coolly.

"No woman in her right mind tells even her best friend when she's been rejected by a good-looking man."

Jill suddenly felt much better, yet surprised that Greg had turned down someone as lovely and charming as Janine. She certainly had all the qualities he looked for in a woman, so why didn't he want her? "He turned you down?" She needed the reassurance badly.

Janine nodded. "He said I'm too much like family. Oh, he didn't hurt my feelings. In fact, I can easily understand what he meant and appreciate the nice way he handled the situation. Greg's one of a kind, Jill. Grab him fast."

"Go home, Janine."

Janine looked around the room. "It would be quite a job tearing out walls and turning the two apartments into one," she remarked lazily. "But the end product would be worth it."

"Janine, go home."

"You're very tense, Jill."

"And you're crazy."

"Just do yourself a favor and think over how you really feel about Greg," Janine advised. "You might be in for a surprise."

Janine left an hour later, the friendship still intact. The two women had mentally skirmished before and would again. They didn't believe in mincing words and would offer their opinions whether wanted or not. Perhaps it was this honesty that kept their friendship solid.

When Jill settled in to bed, she soon learned she wasn't in the mood to sleep. She was too busy remembering how Greg had looked in bed that afternoon. Could he have been right—that the timing had been wrong? Maybe they had rushed it too much. For the past few days the tension between them had been so thick it could have been cut with a knife. Neither could keep their eyes off the other, and each time their gazes clashed, the air grew closer between them. With the frustration building between them, there could only have been one conclusion. It was a shame it hadn't worked out.

Jill rolled onto her side and plumped her pillow. Funny, deep down she knew that any man she had been with hadn't compared with Greg, and it was quite easy to figure out why. Greg gave a woman more than his body; he gave her all he had to give of himself. But, her mind asked her, did he do that with every woman or just her?

"I'm certainly not going to ask his previous lovers for a reference!" Jill shocked herself by speaking her thoughts out loud. She pulled the covers higher, turned the electric blanket up a notch and rolled over again. For one insane moment she thought of indulging in some healthy primal scream therapy.

The following morning Jill and Greg were just one happy family again.

"The scene won't work," Greg argued when Jill gave him the typed pages of an idea they had discussed earlier.

"Why not?" she demanded, aware that there was nothing wrong with the scene, only with Greg.

131

"The dialogue is too inane," he said scornfully. "Jill, even kids between the ages of five and ten wouldn't talk to a gorilla this way. The boy here doesn't sound like a normal kid, and Harry sounds as if he just came out of the jungle."

Jill's face brightened. "Of course." She tapped her forefinger against her lips. "You are so right, Greg. No gorilla should sound as if he grew up in a jungle."

Greg gnashed his teeth. He had thought everything would be settled between them by now. If he had read his horoscope yesterday morning, he would have remained in bed all day—alone. How could he have known that the stars had predicted, "Dark clouds hover over you today. Beware of initiating new relationships because they could turn on you."

"No kidding." Greg had muttered after reading the prediction. He had then read Jill's horoscope, to discover hers had been just as gloomy. It had definitely not been their day.

Jill fiddled with the webbed belt over her purple cotton tunic. "You are really turning into someone I don't know and don't like," she said with sterling clarity. She carefully picked up the papers on Greg's desk and threw them at him. Determined to act the part of the responsible adult of this team, she lifted her chin and stared at him coolly. "I'll go through the scene again and see what can be reworked. Of course, as I'm sure you know, perfection shouldn't be tampered with." With a haughty toss of her head, she exited the room with Greg's profane oaths ringing in her ears.

The tension was back, but this time it wasn't necessarily the sexual variety; it was a combination of anger, desire and even sorrow that their usually

132

amiable working relationship had taken an abrupt turn.

One morning Jill overheard Greg talking on the phone to one of his former girlfriends, making a luncheon appointment with her.

"How quickly we forget," she murmured, staring at the wall across the room.

Greg wasn't too pleased with himself either. While Elaine had been only too happy to see him again, he wasn't one of the most charming lunch companions.

"You need to straighten your life out, Greg," she advised softly when he dropped her off back at her office. "When you know where you're going, give me a call." She kissed him on the cheek and stepped out of the car. The tall, red-haired woman didn't look back as she entered the building.

"Damn!" He slapped his palm against the steering wheel. "Now she's even ruining my love life!"

Greg didn't return to the office for the rest of the afternoon. He drove over to Golden Gate Park and spent several hours wandering through the aquarium. When he left, rain was falling in solid sheets. He wasn't any happier to discover that his car battery was dead. That meant another delay before he could drive home and change into dry clothes.

When he finally arrived home he noticed that Jill's car was gone. Greg frowned, not liking the idea of her out in such bad weather.

Greg decided it might be a good time to do some editing on the current manuscript. It also gave him a good excuse to remain downstairs to see what time Jill came home.

"She just got out of the hospital," he muttered, conveniently forgetting that Jill had had her final checkup a week ago and been pronounced fit to resume all activities. "If she suffers a relapse, I won't become her personal nurse." He slapped a three-ring binder down so hard on the desk that loose papers flew up and drifted down to the floor.

Greg took the time to fix himself a sandwich and coffee before returning downstairs with a mug and an insulated coffee decanter. He didn't work as much as he kept an eye on the clock. By the time he heard the muted whine of the garage door opener, Jill's Trans Am purring to a stop, the slam of the car door and the garage door closing, Greg noted the time: eleven o'clock. He rapidly sat up in his chair and feigned interest in the paper he held.

"Hey, you don't get paid overtime around here." Jill appeared in the doorway. She shrugged off her tan raincoat to reveal a ragged bright pink sweatshirt over a yellow-and-orange-striped leotard and gray nylon parachute pants.

"It must have been some date." Greg's eyes were cold chips, his voice cutting.

"I went to my dance class." Jill couldn't understand the reason for his glacial greeting.

"Dance class! What are you trying to do, kill yourself?" he insisted on knowing. "You've had major surgery not all that long ago and you're out doing things to your body that are impossible."

He's concerned about me, she thought even as she assured him, "I took it easy tonight, but we have a performance coming up soon and I have a lot of catching up to do." She gave a half laugh. "My muscles are reminding me that I'm not used to this, so I'm going upstairs to relax in a hot bath. But why are you down here?" she asked curiously.

Greg shuffled the papers on his desk in order to mask his concern. While part of him wanted to pull her into his arms and carry her upstairs, he also wanted to throttle her for returning to her dancing so soon.

Jill felt the cold vibrations reaching out to her from across the room and didn't like it. He was angry at her, while he had spent all afternoon with Elaine! "How was your lunch?" Her tone implied more than just eating food.

He ignored her pointed remark. "Where are the new pages for Harry working with the elves? Can't you keep anything where it can be found?"

Jill's set features were an indicator of her tightly controlled anger. "Since I don't keep track of the mess on your desk, I wouldn't know," she replied coldly.

"Damnit, Jill, we have a deadline!" Greg roared, alert to the acid eating through his stomach due to the savage way he was treating her, all because she had gone to a class she had been attending for the past three years. The knowledge didn't stop him from tearing her to pieces. "Or do you plan to live off your royalties for the rest of your life and let me do the work?"

Jill's eyes shot icy spears at Greg's heart. "Don't take your temper out on me just because Elaine turned you down for an afternoon fling. That's what she did, didn't she?"

Greg stood there clenching his hands at his sides because if he didn't he would curl them around Jill's neck and squeeze. Without a word he turned away and stomped out of the office. Jill sighed and collapsed against the doorjamb. A few moments later she trudged upstairs in anticipation of a long hot bath. Instead she chose the shower, allowing the hot water to pound into her sore muscles. Jill hadn't overabused her body, but she had worked it harder than she had in many weeks. Standing under the shower, she thought back to her arrival home and Greg's reaction. She wanted to smile at his affronted features, but the reminder of his rage canceled her tender feelings toward the aggravating man.

Jill stepped out of the shower, toweling herself off and patting on dusting powder before slipping on a nightgown and robe. She pulled back her comforter and slid between the sheets. She had just settled in when a nasty thought occurred to her. She jumped out of bed and tore out of her apartment, running down the stairs to the office. She switched the desk lamp on and rummaged through the papers on Greg's desk.

"Bingo," she whispered in triumph.

Jill ascended the stairs leading to Greg's apartment and opened the front door. She was glad to find the interior dark. She had no problem skirting the living room furniture as she silently made her way to the bedroom.

Standing in the doorway, she groped for the light switch. A flick of her hand brought the room to dazzling brilliance.

Greg shot up in bed, as if a bomb had exploded under his bed.

"Wh-what?" He stared at Jill, unable to comprehend her presence.

"Greg! I found the pages!" she exclaimed, presenting him with a bright smile as she held up the papers.

Jill spun on her heel and left the room without bothering to turn off the light.

CHAPTER EIGHT

The next morning Jill was awakened by a knock on her door. She slowly surfaced from a wonderful dream to find out that the sound wasn't coming from the front door but her bedroom door. Greg stood in the doorway, holding a teak breakfast tray that Jill recognized as hers. An enticing aroma wafted from the dishes on the tray.

"What's this?" She squinted, since her eyes refused to open very far.

"An apology." Greg offered her a tentative smile. He entered the room and set the tray in her lap.

Jill sat up and looked down at the dishes holding scrambled eggs, six pieces of bacon, and three warm cinnamon rolls. The smell of hot coffee next caught her attention.

"Nothing's burned." She looked stunned, not only at his peace offering but that nothing sported a charcoal coating. Greg wasn't known for his culinary talents. He was more proficient ordering a meal in a French restaurant than cooking the simplest foods.

"It took a dozen eggs before I got it right," Greg explained sheepishly, sitting down in the chair.

"Why don't you get some coffee for yourself?" Jill suggested, accepting not just the meal but his apology.

"Sounds good." He jumped out of the chair, looking grateful that she wasn't going to throw him out.

Jill nibbled on a piece of bacon, which was a trifle overdone, and sampled her scrambled eggs, somewhat runny but edible. The store-bought cinnamon rolls meant to be baked at home were a little doughy in the center but good all the same. Jill smiled at the idea of Greg slaving over a hot stove fixing her breakfast.

He soon returned with a steaming mug and settled back in the cushioned chair.

"Everything all right?" he inquired anxiously.

"Fine." She handed him a slice of bacon. "I can't possibly eat all this, so I hope you don't mind helping me out."

"Jill, I acted like a perfect ass last night." He sat hunched forward, his palms cradling the warm mug. "I, well, I wasn't in the best of moods. I spent the afternoon at the museum and came out to a dead battery. When I finally got back and you still weren't home, my bad mood just intensified because I didn't know where you had gone. It's been so long since you attended your dance class, I forgot all about it." He smiled wryly. "Of course you certainly found a good way to get back at me. I couldn't get back to sleep for over an hour."

"You made me so mad I was tempted to do much worse," she admitted. "Actually it served you right."

Greg sipped his coffee and set the mug to one side. "We can't ignore what's happened, Jill." He caught her hand in his. "Okay, so we ended up feeling as if it had been our first time and we weren't sure what to do, but there was still something electric between us," he insisted fiercely, leaning forward. "You can't deny it."

"Oh, Greg," she whispered, shaking her head, saddened by the fervor in his voice for something that couldn't be. "We've already broken a rule we set up a long time ago because we both unconsciously knew it just wouldn't work for us. Deep down we knew we couldn't afford to jeopardize our working relationship and friendship for a certain number of nights in bed and eventually a fizzled love affair. We think too much of each other for that."

His insides twisted when Jill blithely dismissed the idea of them having an affair; he found himself wanting so much more than a few hours in bed with her. In fact, if he cared to be brutal with himself and admit it, he was in love with the little witch. It certainly explained why he never stayed long with any of the other women; they weren't Jill. And here she acted as if what they had shared was over before it even had a chance to begin. Wrong! He'd just have to make sure to change her mind on that score. A moment of fast thinking gave him another idea of how to handle the situation.

"Then wouldn't we be better off staying together as lovers?" he recommended off handedly, releasing her hand and sprawling back in the chair, bracing his ankle over one knee. "We always get along." He grimaced at her dry expression. "Okay, we *usually* get along. The past few days have been due to our stars circling in the wrong orbit and your chartreuse aura clashing with my puce one. Now everything should be pretty well smoothed out."

Why did Jill find Greg's suggestion understandable? Easy; because she'd never felt as comfortable with any man, not even Josh, as she did with Greg.

After all, he had seen her at her best and, more important, at her worst. They had shared many meals and late-night snacks over the years and probably knew more about each other than many couples who had been married for years. She admitted their first time as lovers had lacked a vital spark, but that could happen to anyone, couldn't it? At the same time the question nagging her was, what if Greg was wrong? What if they weren't meant to share a physical relationship?

"Are you sure you're not saying all this just to get me into bed and have your way with me?" she asked archly.

Greg looked smug. "I wouldn't have far to go right now."

Jill felt the heat start at her toes and creep slowly up her body under Greg's searching gaze. Instead of retreating under the covers, she found herself sitting up a bit straighter before realizing that all she had accomplished was to inadvertently pull her teddy's neckline down until it uncovered most of her breasts. If she took too deep a breath, she'd be totally lost. She picked up her fork and concentrated on finishing her eggs. She tore a corner off one of the cinnamon rolls and popped it into her mouth.

"What, no comeback?" Greg asked lightly.

"I don't want to bring on any indigestion," she tossed back with a smile.

Having gotten his point across, Greg picked up his coffee mug and stood. "I'll let you finish your breakfast in peace. Since I gave you hell last night, I figured the least I could do is surprise you with breakfast in bed." His storm-gray eyes sparkled wickedly. "I'm only sorry I couldn't share it with you properly." With a jaunty wave of the hand he sauntered out.

After Jill finished her meal she carried the tray back to the kitchen. The scene that greeted her was enough to ruin any meal.

A microwave pan filled with congealed bacon grease sat on the kitchen counter next to a frying pan colored with yellow and brown bits of dried egg. The butter dish now held half-melted butter, and the coffee maker filter dripped stains into the sink over an even dozen broken eggshells. Greg hadn't been kidding.

Jill vowed she would get even with him after she finished cleaning up the disaster area facing her.

By the time she had cleaned up the kitchen, showered and dressed, her anger over Greg leaving the mess to her had abated a bit, but not enough.

She arrived downstairs prepared to inform Greg that she didn't appreciate his leaving a kitchen resembling a major war zone only to find his office door closed and the faint click of computer keys reaching her ears. She reluctantly obeyed his unspoken request for privacy and settled down to her own work.

Three long hours later Jill was positive the crick in her neck was a permanent condition, but after viewing all the work she had accomplished, she wasn't about to complain about a little discomfort. She had polished the scenes she and Greg had discussed a few days before and began to run the printer for the two copies they would need to go over it again.

"Ah, the marvels of modern science." She dropped an affectionate pat on the purring computer terminal.

Jill stood and stretched her arms over her head

and rolled her shoulders before dropping her arms toward the floor with her back kept flat. She closed her eyes, willing each tense muscle to relax.

"That won't work and you know it." Arms slid around her waist and lifted her before a pair of hands descended on her shoulders, kneading the tense skin expertly.

"Mmm," Jill crooned in bliss, feeling the tension flow out of her body under Greg's touch. "Such wonderful hands you have, Grandma."

"You really should get in the hot tub," Greg suggested, halting his massage and pushing her blond curls aside to bestow a light kiss on her nape. His mouth lingered there a fraction of a second more. "That would do you even more good."

Jill's eyes flew open at the soft caress. It shouldn't have sent a strange feeling to her stomach, as if the bottom had dropped out. After all, how many times had he kneaded her aching muscles and dropped a kiss on her head or shoulder afterward? How many times had he recommended she use the hot tub, not to mention the times they had shared it? This kiss was most definitely not the same, though, and only her feminine instinct would agree with her illogical argument.

"Sounds good to me." There was a hollow ring to her reply. "I got all the polishing done and ran off two copies." She gestured blindly to her desk.

Greg hid his smile of triumph. The lady was definitely capitulating. She just didn't know it yet. "Meet you out back in ten minutes?"

Jill nodded. Deep down, she knew there was more than a relaxing hour in the hot, swirling water coming up. She just wondered if she was truly ready for it. If she didn't want anything to happen, she would only have to tell him she would go upstairs and take a hot shower instead. She didn't say another word.

The spa had been bought a year and a half ago to help Greg's bad back. Jill had also found it useful after an exhausting dance class. So that it could be used all year round, it had been installed inside a greenhouse that jutted out the back of the house, where a large kitchen used to be. Tropical plants, stereo speakers and padded chaise lounges added to an erotic atmosphere.

When Jill arrived in the glass-enclosed room, Greg was already there checking the water temperature.

"It's just right," he announced, not bothering to turn around.

"How did you know I was here?" Jill queried.

He straightened and turned around, flashing her a grin. "I have eyes in the back of my head."

She affected a theatrical pout. "And here I thought it was something exotic, such as a tiny camera hidden behind your left ear." She grasped the hem of her oversize t-shirt and pulled it up over her head.

Greg's mouth went dry. "Whe-when did you get that?" he croaked, gesturing to the tiny scraps of turquoise-and-black-striped cotton fabric barely covering her vital areas.

"When I went to Hawaii last year."

Greg stepped abruptly down into the water to hide what could prove to be a threatening embarrassment.

"Want something to drink?" Jill headed for the small refrigerator hidden in a corner of the room.

Greg thought of the bottle of champagne chilling

in the interior. "You choose." Jill's squeal told him she'd found his surprise.

"Why, Mr. Richmond, are you trying to seduce me?" She danced over to the edge of the spa carrying the bottle and two plastic wineglasses. Jill manipulated the cork and poured a small amount into each glass. "We both know alcohol and spas don't mix, so I figure our one glass per person will last longer if I only pour a little bit at a time," she explained, handing him the glass and sliding down into the heated water. She rested her head against the edge and allowed the water jets to pound into her back. A lazy smile touched her lips as she watched Greg through half-closed eyes. "If you don't mind, I think I'll spend the rest of the year here."

"You're out of luck. We've got a book to finish."

"I'll work from here." She sipped her champagne, stretching her legs out across the width of the spa until her foot grazed something. Greg gave a savage oath as he jumped back. "Greg, I'm so sorry," she gasped, coming to attention after realizing what she had done. She waded over to him, prepared to offer comfort. "Did I hurt you?"

He thrust his hands through his hair and laughed harshly. "I'm beginning to believe you have something against me." He looked up at the ceiling as he spoke.

"Want me to kiss it better?"

Jill's softly spoken question caught Greg's attention with full force. His head whipped around to face her, seeing her limpid eyes, flushed cheeks and trembling lips.

"If I recall correctly, you said we could never work if we were having an affair," he said roughly, unwilling to believe what he had heard and what he now saw.

She shook her head, unable to give him a reasonable answer. Jill only knew that she had ignored her inner feelings too long and now acted on impulse. She moved closer until she stood between his legs, feeling his rough skin caress her own smooth limbs. Capturing his gaze, she reached behind her neck and untied the strings, letting them fall down over her breasts. The strings behind her back were next released. Two triangles of fabric drifted down to the swirling water, rapidly disappearing to the edge of the tub.

Greg swallowed in the hope of easing the sand coating his throat. No such luck. What he had seen that day in the dim light of his bedroom couldn't compare with the beauty standing before him with the afternoon sun warming her bare skin. Her lightly tanned flesh seemed to grow under his ardent gaze. Without uttering a word he reached out and pulled her to him on the molded plastic bench. His mouth claimed hers with a hunger she eagerly reciprocated.

"You taste so sweet," he muttered, bathing her lips with his moisture. "Jill, give yourself to me."

"Kiss me," she pleaded, kneeling in the water and clinging to him. Her lips fluttered over his chin and along his jaw.

"That and more." His vow washed over her like a warm breeze. He curled an arm around her hips and drew her up to him. They whispered loving praise, nibbled, stroked and loved with their lips. Greg's fingertips traced the delicate lines of her shoulders and skimmed down her sides, just barely grazing her breasts. When he reached her hips, he moved back up to the sensitive hollow of her throat.

145

"Greg," Jill moaned, burying her face against his neck and nipping him none too gently in punishment.

"Oh, no." He chuckled, now making a wide sweep of her back with his hands. "We're not rushing our loving one bit. There's not going to be any regrets this time. We're going to experience something never beheld by the human race."

She drew back slightly, searching his face for a sign that this wasn't just an afternoon dalliance for him. She knew it wasn't for her. She mapped out his upper chest with inquisitive fingertips, following those paths with her lips, tasting the faint tangy flavor of chlorine misting his skin.

Greg cupped her buttocks, pulling her up onto his lap. His arousal swelled under her hip. One hand slid under the elastic band of her bikini bottoms and stroked her satiny skin. He delved further, finding her moist and ready for him. With each probe of his fingers, Jill moaned against his skin.

"Does this tell you how much I want you?" he whispered, pressing butterfly kisses over her eyes and down her nose to her mouth.

Jill parted her lips under his marauding tongue, but it wasn't enough. She whimpered, rubbing her sensitive breasts against the crinkly hair covering his chest and pressing her mouth harder against his. The tip of her tongue dipped into his mouth to gather in his taste and warmth. Yet it still wasn't enough. She pressed her hand against his chest, measuring the rapid beat against her own, and trailed her fingers down to his waist and below.

"Easy, sweetheart." He caught hold of her earlobe with his teeth. "As I said, we're taking our time if it kills us."

"It just may destroy me," she replied.

Greg slid his hands under the minuscule bikini briefs and pushed them downward. Once they floated free, he started to lift her up so he could see all of her.

"Greg, please." The pained expression on her face alerted him to some sort of agony.

"What's wrong?" he asked, wondering what could be troubling her.

She offered him a weak smile. "I—well, before I didn't think about it because the room was dark, but now . . ." Her voice trailed off as she looked to one side.

Greg cupped her chin with one hand and gently turned her to face him. "Your face is flushed and you look ready to cry, but I'm not sure what brought it on," he pressed.

Jill licked her lips. "My scar is so ugly," she finally blurted. "I don't want you to see it and become repulsed."

Greg's eyes softened to the misty gray of late morning fog. "And you thought that would put me off?" he chided. "Oh, Jill, your scar is part of you and certainly nothing ugly to me." To prove his point he lifted her higher until her lower torso was level with his face and he saw the reddish scar slashing across the pearly skin. He glanced up to see her eyes closed tightly, fearing the worst. Wanting nothing more than to reassure her, he leaned forward, caressing the faint ridge with his mouth, then moved lower. He listened to her throaty moans as he loved her until her body shook with spasms of joy.

"I want you, love," he whispered, pressing another intimate kiss against her when she finally stilled. "But when we make love, I don't intend to drown during our climax." He stood up and swept

147

her into his arms, then hesitated long enough to throw a towel around Jill and himself.

"Wait." She gestured for him to bend down so she could grab the champagne bottle.

Greg stopped at the door. "My place or yours?"

Jill's tongue snaked around his ear. "Is Mrs. Hathaway cleaning yours or mine?"

Greg thought for a moment. "Mine."

Jill's tongue now darted inside the curved orifice. "Well, then, we don't want a third party hanging around, do we?"

He agreed wholeheartedly with that. Greg wasted no time in climbing the stairs to Jill's apartment. She leaned down to turn the doorknob and push the door open. Greg headed for the bedroom and dropped Jill onto the bed.

"Greg!" she squealed, bouncing on the firm mattress.

"Jill!" he mocked, dropping down beside her. He whisked the towels off their damp bodies and tossed them to the floor. He half lay over her, his fingers tunneling through her hair. He smiled down at her. "Congratulate us, Jilly Bean," he murmured. "We haven't yelled at each other for several hours now."

"I never wanted to yell at you, Greg," she confessed, mimicking his caress. "Sometimes I feel like two different people, one of them a horrible shrew."

"Frustration does that to a person." He nuzzled the vulnerable hollow of her throat. "At least I know why you've been so cranky. And here I thought it was some woman's thing."

Jill reared back at his teasing taunt. "Why, you chauvinist—"

Her words were smothered under his invading mouth, and she gave up without a battle. She

148

hugged his waist and rubbed her calves along his thighs until she reached the warmth she knew to be seeking her. Now every inch of her body was covered by his heat.

They kissed as if time were running out on them, and they feasted with an insatiable hunger, speaking in murmured love words.

Laughing softly, Jill pushed Greg onto his back and straddled his body. She trailed a line of kisses along his breastbone and down the narrow line of hair leading to his flat stomach. She caressed him with love and tenderness, only pausing to glance up and smile at the sounds of his pleasured groans. There soon came a time when he couldn't stand any more of her sensual torture. He pulled her up and over him, his legs nudging hers apart. Their eyes met and spoke messages that said so very much before Jill arched her back at the same time Greg thrust upward into her silken heat. Jill cried with pleasure, causing Greg to hesitate.

"Am I hurting you?" he asked, cupping his hands over her hips, holding her tightly against him.

"No," she whispered, twisting frantically to keep him deep within her. "Don't stop, Greg, love me."

He complied easily, their bodies melding into one unit.

"You're burning me, Jill," he spoke hoarsely.

"I'm the one on fire." She fitted herself to his rhythm. The tiny coil inside her unraveled, building upward, upward until Jill stood on top of a volcano. The scorching heat came from Greg as he accelerated his pace.

Jill panted, silently ordering her lungs to take in more oxygen to combat the lightheaded feeling that left her so free. Her hips rose and fell in perfect cadence, and Greg felt her growing tension.

149

"Come with me, babe," he urged, twisting his lower body and thrusting until she cried with pleasure. "Let yourself go and climb as high as you can."

Her eyes widened with the passion exploding in her body. "I—can't."

"Sure you can. Trust me. We'll have the world, sweetheart. We'll have it all." Beads of sweat glistened on his forehead as he exercised control over the screaming demands of his body. "Don't worry, you'll go with me all the way."

And she did. Jill clung to Greg, allowing the tidal wave to sweep them both out until they were left gasping for air. She lay still, warm in his embrace, wishing it could go on forever.

"Mmm, now I know why all your girlfriends were always smiling," she teased, rubbing her nose against his. "Why, Greg, you're blushing!"

"Cut it out, Jill." He shifted uneasily.

"Are you embarrassed that I'm talking about your sexual prowess?" she asked, slipping off him to lie curled up at his side. "I like your prowess . . . a lot."

"Damnit, Jill, you're making me sound like some sex object," he grumbled, pulling her even closer.

"Hmm, a sex object." She nibbled kisses on his flat brown nipple that soon peaked under her ministration. "I like that, too."

"Greedy witch," he accused, but his husky voice gave her another idea.

"Yes, but only for you." Her hand stroked tantalizingly over him.

"And that's the way it should be." Greg soon took over finishing what Jill had started.

Several hours later they toasted each other with

150

warm flat champagne and made love to each other again.

"I'll fix the toast," Jill announced the next morning. "You always burn it. Would you get the peanut butter out, please?"

"On toast?" Greg grimaced. "English muffins, yes, but not on toast."

"Toast is just a square English muffin." She leaned over to plant a smacking kiss on his lips. It was a few moments before they resumed their meal preparations.

"What is this stuff?" Greg held up a small plastic container he had found in the refrigerator. The dark brown contents didn't look appetizing.

Jill glanced over and returned to her task. "Chocolate peanut butter. It's really good."

"It looks nauseating." He quickly returned the plastic tub to the refrigerator.

"Candy bars are made of chocolate and peanuts. It's the same thing." Jill dished the eggs onto two plates. "It tastes great on sugar cookies."

"You eat too much junk food," Greg told her. "I don't understand how you can eat like that and not weigh four hundred pounds."

"Dance class burns a lot of calories, as do a few other activities." She winked saucily.

Greg and Jill had shared many breakfasts before, but never with Jill seated on his lap and feeding him choice tidbits from her plate. And that was the way Mrs. Hathaway found them when she walked into the apartment an hour later. Jill wore a pink chemise that matched her blush, and Greg's only apparel was a towel draped around his hips.

"M-Mrs. Hathaway," Jill stammered, jumping up

from Greg's lap, looking like an errant schoolgirl caught in a flagrant act by the principal.

"Well," the older woman said with a sniff, "it's about time." She marched back into the living room muttering under her breath.

Jill and Greg looked at each other, finding it difficult to keep their faces straight and their laughter contained. When they heard the front door open and close, they finally broke into gales of laughter.

"Did you see her face?" Jill gasped, resting her face against Greg's neck. Their bodies shook with mirth.

"She certainly didn't act as shocked as I thought she would." He had trouble keeping his voice steady. He looked down at the towel barely covering his hips. "Maybe you'd better run over to my place and pick up some clothes for me. Of course, after what she said and saw, I don't think anything we do can shock her."

"Um." Jill looked down at what the towel did show. "What a shame. She'll miss the sight of a lifetime." She kissed him, savoring the taste of coffee on his lips. "On second thought, I don't want to share you with anyone. I'll get dressed and find some clothes for you among that mess you call a closet."

"Want some help with zippers and buttons?" He leered at her.

She shook her head. "No way. With your idea of helping, I'd end up not wearing a stitch. Tell you what, though, you can help me by cleaning up the kitchen." She danced out of his reach.

Once they had both dressed and adjourned downstairs, they sat in Greg's office going over their work.

"We're way behind schedule," Greg announced,

holding up the finished chapters, a pile that looked pitifully thin.

"Our arguments took up valuable time," Jill murmured, glancing through the spiral-bound notebook filled with scenes, ideas and brief summaries of each chapter.

He sighed heavily. "Yeah, it's been rough on both of us," he agreed. He stretched his legs out in front of him, ankles crossed. "We've got a lot of work ahead of us."

She shrugged. "That's never scared us before." She glanced down, idly tracing the screen-printed image of Hairy Harry on her pale blue sweatshirt. That along with black nylon parachute pants and thick yellow wool socks made up her outfit. The sides of her hair had been clipped back from her face, and she continually lifted her hair and let it fall back down in soft tangles. A wicked twinkle brightened her eyes. "It just means that we have to work nights and not schedule any heavy dates. You'd better go through your black book and tell your ladies you won't be available for a while."

"Okay." Greg turned to his phone and dialed.

Jill couldn't believe what she was seeing. He had actually taken her joke seriously and was calling the many women he had gone out with. She thought briefly of killing him. Before she could say anything, her telephone rang.

"Excuse me," she said stiffly, jumping to her feet. "If that's Tom Selleck asking me for a date, I'll be sure to tell him I'm tied up for the next couple of weeks." She walked into her office and picked up the receiver. "Hello?"

"Darling, I hope I'm not disturbing you." Greg's voice was as smooth as well-aged brandy. "I'm afraid I've got a lot of work ahead of me, so we won't be able to see each other for a while. I really hate to do this to you, but it's for the best, because I know if I had you alone I'd want to do wicked and lascivious things to your body."

"I—" Jill spun around to see Greg's grinning face as he stood in the doorway of his office.

"Don't worry, I'll make it up to you later." His voice lowered to a seductive level, letting her know exactly how he intended to do that.

She slammed the phone down and ran back into Greg's office. "You devil!" She pummeled him with her fists.

Laughing, he locked his hands behind her waist and lifted her to his eye level. Their mouths met and melted together. Greg pulled his head away, breathing harshly. "Ever make it on a desk?"

Jill's fingertips pressed against his chest. "We have work to do," she reminded him primly.

"Don't you think it's time for a coffee break?" Greg asked hopefully.

She shook her head, knowing if she didn't remain strong now, they'd be upstairs in a matter of minutes. "Besides, Carlysle would demand the exact details of why we were late with our book, and you know how he can sniff out lies."

He sighed heavily. "Okay, party pooper, but you'd better be prepared to finish this book in record time."

Jill linked her arms around his neck and kissed him on the nose. "Don't worry, darling, you'll be a better man for it," she vowed in sugary tones.

Greg didn't look so sure. He had only received a taste of Jill's love, and his hunger had increased after the appetizer. He wanted more than she could imagine giving to him. Only time would settle his lusty appetite, if it could ever be satisfied.

CHAPTER NINE

"Take it easy, Janine!" Greg pleaded even as the dark-haired woman dragged him into the dance center's large auditorium. "You're practically pulling my arm out of the socket."

"Don't you dare start complaining now." She selected two seats five rows from the front and deposited him in the second seat from the aisle. The only way he could escape now was over her. "Jill is counting on you attending her performance, and I'm making sure you don't try to sneak out. You can't disappoint her now."

Greg groaned, resting his head against the top of the metal chair with a thin square of vinyl on the seat in place of padding. He certainly wasn't going to pretend that he had any heartfelt desire to be here. He turned his head and gazed at Janine with undisguised temper.

"Greg," she crooned, patting his hand, "think of this as a family duty."

He made a rude noise. "My family duty meant visiting Aunt Letitia every Sunday afternoon. It ended when I was ten and decided to fill in the roses on her wallpaper with my purple marker. If I hadn't done it, I would probably still be going there."

Janine rolled her eyes in exasperation. "With all the hours Jill spent in rehearsal and preparing her costumes, you *will* enjoy this show," she hissed just as the overhead lights blinked once in warning and lowered.

Greg settled back in his seat, his hands comfortably clasped across his stomach. He watched a tall, gangly woman step onto the stage and listened to her welcome speech to parents and friends attending Oaktree Dance Academy's spring program. He sighed deeply, earning a dark glare from Janine. He had an idea it was going to be a long evening.

He tuned the woman's words out and thought back over the past few weeks. Nothing had truly prepared him for the happiness Jill had given him. Every night they had slept in each other's arms, and each day they had worked hard on their book. If they had been in tune before, now they definitely shared a blending of the minds. Their writing flowed together so well, they had finished the book well ahead of schedule and had recently begun plans for a new one. Greg had continued teasing Jill about her dance classes and her hours of rehearsal, but he had never shared his fears with her. What if she wasn't ready for all the additional physical exertion a performance must demand? He knew he couldn't stand to see her in pain again.

For the past two weeks Jill had been asking him to attend the dance performance, but he had never given her an affirmative answer. In his mind's eye a dance recital conjured images of red-cheeked little girls dressed in pastel leotards and tutus, attempting faltering dance steps on a stage. Only the hurt disappointment he had glimpsed on Jill's face and in her eyes had prompted him to agree to be there. Janine had picked him up to ensure that he didn't find a way to back out of attending.

"When does Jill come on?" he asked, only to be shushed by someone seated behind them.

"The second and the last numbers," Janine murmured, keeping her eyes on the stage.

Greg stared up at the ceiling. He leaned over and whispered in her ear. "How many numbers do we have to suffer through?"

"Five and shut up."

Greg shifted uneasily in his seat. Perhaps he could catch a quick nap.

The first dance consisted of six small girls between the ages of four and six, looking adorable dressed in colorful costumes resembling flowers and fairies. They concentrated on stepping and sliding to *The Sugar Plum Fairy*.

Greg stifled a yawn, and Janine, seeing his sign of boredom, jabbed him in the ribs.

"Don't you dare fall asleep," she muttered her dire warning.

Not soon enough for Greg, the curtain closed on the flowers and fairies amid polite applause. The mistress of ceremonies returned to the front of the stage and explained that the young junior class, ages seven and eight, would perform the *Sorcerer's Apprentice* with advanced dancer Jill Blake's assistance as the hapless apprentice.

The heavy curtains slowly parted along the dark stage. The lights remained dim to reveal a dark cavern. A figure dressed in black moved across the boards to the first haunting strains of the music. When the dancer turned to face the audience, Greg sat up a little straighter.

The dancer's clothing might have been black, but her aura was pure sun and moonlight as far as Greg was concerned.

The audience chuckled as the timid apprentice

157

cautiously approached her master's coned hat sitting on a table in the middle of the stage. She moved forward, then swiftly backed off, showing wariness in the lines of her body. She used a great deal of body language to explain to the audience how badly she wanted to wear her master's hat. Suddenly, the hat "magically" appeared on her head with a pearlized light glowing around her head to indicate her great magical power. Papers danced in the air, as did "clay" pots as the power grew along with the apprentice's bravado. There was nothing she couldn't do, thanks to the magic hat.

A wave of her hand brought a tiny broom leaning against the wall upright. The broom's costume was constructed of brown cloth, with the performer's two legs cunningly hidden by false bristles.

With another wave of the hand the broom was ordered to sweep the cavern. The now-saucy apprentice danced lively steps around the room, then stopped, palm cradling her chin in thought. A snap of the fingers, a waggle of the hands, and the broom multiplied into three brooms. The apprentice was so pleased with her magic that she settled in a large chair, her hands continuing to wave the brooms into action. It wasn't long before her tasks tired her. She yawned, laid her head back and fell asleep, her hands still waving about. She slept on, unaware that her magic continued to multiply the small brooms as they performed their task with energetic zeal. Soon the stage was covered with dancing brooms which developed more mischief than work. The apprentice slept on until a bright light from the cavern stairs shone on her face. She bounced up, looking appropriately apologetic for getting caught by her master. She carefully replaced the hat on the table, the brooms quickly decreased in number and the apprentice was soon dejectedly sweeping the floor.

Greg continued staring at the stage after the curtains closed.

"What did you think of Jill?" Janine broke into his trance.

He coughed, clearing his throat of the lump there. "I never knew," he murmured, in awe of what he had just witnessed. He sat slightly forward, waiting for the last routine.

The last number included the advanced jazz class dancing to a modern rock tune. The ten women wore red sequined two-piece leotards and sheer red tights. The energy expended in the routine was phenomenal and electrifying to the audience.

Greg couldn't keep his eyes off Jill. He found himself wanting her so much he ached.

When the number was finished he jumped up, applauding loudly until Janine pulled him back down in his seat.

"I see you didn't fall asleep," she said with a smirk.

"Janine, with you around, a statue wouldn't be able to sleep," he retorted.

"I'll ignore that," Janine said loftily, standing up and grabbing his hand. "Come on, let's greet the star."

Backstage, Jill stood in one corner talking to some of the women she had danced with. She had put leg warmers and a ragged sweatshirt on for warmth. Her hair, which had been caught back by red barrettes, gleamed under the hot lights. A faint sheen of perspiration glistened on her brow and around her mouth. Just then Jill turned and saw Greg. Her lips moved in a heart-stopping smile as she sprinted across the area and leaped into his arms.

"You came, you came," she murmured over and over, hugging him tightly. Her face and eyes were alive with the happiness she felt. "Oh, Greg, I'm so glad you're here." She grasped his face and kissed him.

Shame clung to his conscience as he recalled all his arguments for not wanting to attend. He hadn't realized until then how important his presence was to her.

"You look great," he said once he'd regained use of his mouth.

"I did her makeup," Janine piped up proudly.

Greg shot her a look filled with exasperation. "Actually I was talking about her dancing," he shot back.

"Okay, you two." Jill took Greg's arm, pressing it against her side. "I'm glad you came," she said happily, leading him to a group of people. "There are some people I want you to meet."

For the next hour Jill led Greg from one group to another, introducing him to fellow students and the instructors.

"So you're Jill's writing partner." A tall, voluptuous brunette edged Greg away from the group. Her green almond-shaped eyes were as hard as gemstones. "Funny, you don't look like a children's-book writer." The tip of her tongue appeared to bathe her lower lip. If Greg had seen Jill do that, he would have been aroused immediately. From this woman the action only left him cold. "I could see you writing men's adventure books or those steamy detective novels instead of books for kids. You'd be good." She spoke in a calculated purr. "At a lot of things."

One kind of woman Greg didn't like was the shark; they were the women who hunted their prey, snapped them up and swam on to snare a new victim. No matter how lovely she was, he didn't intend to be the bait for the evening.

"I'll see you at the party." The woman smiled, showing small but slightly sharp teeth. She glided away, but not without brushing her hand across the front of his slacks.

"She eats her men alive, love." Jill appeared at Greg's side, her hand hooking his arm in a possessive grip. "You wouldn't have a chance."

"Give me the benefit of the doubt that my taste is much better than Madame Guillotine." He smiled, snaking his arm around her waist. "You look sexy in that outfit." He lowered his voice. "Good enough to eat."

"The flattery won't work until you tell me what that she-wolf said to you." She couldn't quite carry off her stern expression.

"She said she'd see me at the party. What party is she talking about?" he asked. "And where's Janine?"

"The party is for the dancers and crew, and Janine left a few minutes ago, figuring I'd give you a ride home." Jill looked across the room at the dark-haired temptress. "We don't need to go to the party," she said softly, stroking his arm with the tips of her fingers.

"My thought exactly," Greg murmured.

An hour later Jill sat oohing and ahhing in the hot tub as the water jets massaged her sore muscles. Greg was just content to sprawl on the opposite bench and watch the enticing sight of Jill's bare breasts just below the bubbling water level.

"You're one sexy lady, Jill Blake." His lazy drawl floated in the air. "How can anyone who looks as sexy as you write children's books when you should be starring in a porno movie?"

"A porno film?" She snapped her hand against the top of the water, sending a small wave into his face. "You're really asking for it now!"

"Hey!" His retort was garbled under the splash. "That's playing dirty." He reached out and pulled her to him.

"I've only just begun," she gurgled, sliding her arms around his neck and her legs around his hips.

"Sounds good to me." Greg's respiration grew shallow.

"Same here," Jill replied.

Greg put his hands under her arms and drew her up until her navel was level with his face. "Hm, you've got an innie." He touched his tongue to the delicate indentation. "And I've got an outie. Appropriate, isn't it?" He looked up at her with a wicked arch of the eyebrows.

"Greg!" She couldn't hold back her blush.

He was otherwise occupied brushing his open mouth over her stomach and up to tug on an impudent nipple.

"Did you know that your blush and the color of your nipples is the same?" he mumbled, lapping beads of moisture from the pink nub. "It's not only very enchanting but very tasty, too."

Jill threw back her head, her eyes closed so she could savor the emotions running through her more fully. Soft whimpers sounded from her slightly parted lips, and the stream surrounding her body left tiny incandescent beads on her skin. Her hands gripped his damp shoulders in order to keep her balance as Greg's marauding tongue threatened to send her into another world.

"You do that so well, my love," she breathed, flexing her fingers on his taut skin.

"Did I ever tell you that your skin's as soft as a duck's bottom?" He nibbled along the perimeter of her belly.

"No one can compliment a woman like you can." The last word came out as a low moan.

He kept on tormenting her until the heat of the glass-enclosed room seeped through her pores to create an even greater fever within her. Greg took his time mapping out every inch of sensitive skin before slowly moving up to her breasts. His lips closed over one nipple and pulled on it almost roughly. As before, his patience could last only so long when he loved her. He suckled as eagerly as a newborn infant would to sustain life.

Jill whimpered, whispering entreaties for Greg to end this torture. She bent her head, nipping his ear in punishment for the torment she suffered. "No more," she ordered hoarsely.

Greg bent his head back. "More?"

"Oh!" She pounded him with her fists and managed to drop back into his lap with satisfying ease. With a twist and wiggle of her hips, she welcomed him into herself, creating another whirlpool to battle the one circling them.

Greg gripped Jill's hips and thrust upward. Their eyes met and held, binding them in an enchanted world. Jill's lips were slightly parted as she panted with each forceful thrust. She wrapped her legs around his waist and clung even tighter.

"You're mine, Jill," Greg told her in a rough voice, clasping the sides of her head with his hands and kissing her forcefully. "All mine."

163

"Yes," she whispered in return. "Yes!"

Greg's movements quickened as the exquisite pain caught up with them until they shuddered with release. They remained in each other's arms, unwilling to part just yet.

"Making it in a spa may be considered sexy, but I think I'm of the conservative school, where a bed has all the comforts." Greg stood up, still hugging Jill tightly to him. "Come on, let's find that bed."

Jill hooked her heels at the base of his spine. "Sounds good to me." She yawned, resting her chin on his shoulders.

Greg chuckled. "Lazy witch. Okay, babe, let's go to bed." He carried her upstairs to his apartment and into his bedroom. If he had had any other ideas for the balance of the night, a now sound asleep Jill banished them.

Greg was drinking his third cup of coffee and working busily in his office by the time a heavy-eyed Jill staggered downstairs the next morning.

"Good afternoon," he teased, giving her a warm smile.

"Ugh." She picked up his cup and sipped the hot brew.

"Very good, you're getting more into Harry's role every day."

Jill ran her fingers through her hair. "It's mornings such as this that I can't find myself liking you very much." She dug into the kangaroo pockets of her lilac sweatshirt for her pack of cigarettes and lighter. "Do you have any pages for me to look over?" The small amount of caffeine had helped clear her brain.

Greg nodded, lacing his fingers together and stretching his arms over his head for a much-needed backache relief. "Why don't you get your coffee first?"

Jill agreed as she lit a cigarette and pushed her lighter back into her pocket. She ignored Greg's exaggerated coughs and waves of the arms to banish the imaginary clouds of smoke. She looked out the window but saw only gray mist covering the glass. A soft sigh escaped her lips. "Wouldn't you rather go for a walk in that lovely fog?" she wheedled.

"Wouldn't you rather bank that lovely check we'll receive once this equally lovely book is finished?"

"I'll get my coffee and be right back."

"This can't work," she argued later that day.

"Why not?" Greg looked up from his typing.

"The transition isn't smooth enough," Jill explained, pushing him out of his chair and moving the material backward to the scene she was referring to. "If he's visiting the beach, there has to be more reason for going than just appearing there." She quickly typed in the commands so that she could insert her idea. When she finished, she looked up to where Greg stood behind her. "See, doesn't that make more sense?"

Greg leaned over, one hand on the back of her chair and the other braced on the desk next to the computer terminal. With a mere shift of his weight he could brush his lips across her temple, but he resisted the urge, mainly because he knew one kiss would only lead to another and from there they would end up upstairs in no time.

"Here." He gestured to the flickering amber letters on the black screen. "That sentence needs more punch." He proceeded to show what he meant.

The couple were so engrossed in their work that they didn't pause until the light outside dimmed and they were forced to turn on a lamp in order to see.

"So far, so good." Greg programmed the printer to spew out the chapter they had just finished. "How about dinner and a movie?"

"Sounds fine to me." Jill looked down at her casual clothing. "Give me a half-hour so I can look properly seductive." She lowered her voice to a sultry croon.

"Just as long as you don't look too seductive, or we'll never get out of here." He brushed his fingers across her cheek and followed the caress with his lips, which soon slid down to her mouth.

"Greg?"

"Hmm?"

"If we remain here any longer, we'll have to eat after the movie." She bent her head so he could reach the tender spot where her shoulder met her neck. "And I'm pretty hungry."

"I'll buy you some popcorn at the movies." He inhaled the strawberry scent of her shampoo. He drew back, breathing hard just from that brief caress. "While I'd rather take you upstairs to bed, I'm going to go take a cold shower instead. I'll meet you down here in a half-hour." With one last kiss, he left her.

Jill also took a quick shower, pinned her hair back and applied makeup lightly before dressing in a red sweater and charcoal wool slacks. She grabbed her gray pea coat and ran downstairs to find Greg already waiting for her.

"Maybe I should ravish you instead." He grabbed hold of her hand.

She wrinkled her nose. "I'll hold you to that

promise later." She lightly jabbed her finger against his forest green sweater. "Did you find a movie?"

Greg nodded. "We'll just make it if you don't mind eating afterward."

"Not as long as you keep me sated with popcorn," she answered.

The movie was a comedy that left them with sides aching from laughter. What delighted Jill even more were Greg's erotic comments murmured in her ear about how he planned to recreate the love scenes when they returned home. That was one promise she intended to have him keep!

After the film they walked down the street to a restaurant known for every kind of hamburger imaginable.

"Good evening." The hostess greeted them with a smile. "Would you prefer the smoking or nonsmoking section?"

"Smoking," Jill requested swiftly, without bothering with their usual toss of the coin.

"Nonsmoking," Greg said at the same time.

The waitress was confused by the conflicting replies. "Aren't you two together?" she finally asked.

"Of course," Jill said impatiently, turning to Greg. "Give me a break. I wasn't able to smoke at the movies."

"Then refraining during the meal shouldn't kill you, should it?" he countered pleasantly, then turned back to the hostess. "We'd like nonsmoking, please." He glanced down at Jill. "Show some willpower, will you?"

Her eyes blazed at this slur to her self-control. "Fine." Her reply hung icicles over her head as she swept past him to follow the hostess. She'd show him more willpower than he could ever imagine.

They were seated in a burnt-orange vinyl booth

and handed menus before Jill spoke again. "I gather you're paying?"

Greg counted to ten under his breath. "I think I can afford it." The lady makes me crazy, he thought to himself. If I didn't love her so much I'd probably kill her.

During the short time before the waitress appeared, Jill hummed the movie theme under her breath and fiddled with the small red plastic container holding the sugar and artificial sweetener packets. After they were rearranged to her satisfaction, she played with the salt and pepper shakers. She looked up and smiled when the waitress appeared asking if they were ready to order.

"Yes, I'd like a full order of potato skins with extra bacon and cheese, the guacamole burger, onion rings and a large iced tea." She wrinkled her brows in concentration. "I guess I'll decide on dessert later." She flashed a bright smile at Greg, daring him to say one word about her large order.

"I'll have the Gold Coast burger, fries, and coffee." He sighed. After the waitress left, he leaned across the table and caught one of Jill's hands. "Have I ever told you how exasperating you are?"

"Why, suh, I do declare you're funnin' me," she cooed in a sugary Southern drawl, batting her lashes in true Scarlett O'Hara fashion.

"And it can't be due to sexual frustration," he continued, keeping his voice low.

"That's true—we've certainly taken care of that problem," Jill said pertly, looking up when the waitress set their drinks in front of them and left.

When their food arrived they tucked in with hungry gusto. Jill ended up not only finishing all her food but also ordering lemon meringue pie for dessert.

"Good thing we're walking back to the house." Greg pulled several bills out of his pocket to pay. "Of course, I may have to roll you back to the house."

"Then you'll have all that much more of me to love." She slid her arm around his waist under his corduroy jacket. "Why don't we stop off for a drink at Mahoney's?"

"Sounds good to me. I'll even let you pay." He curved a hand over her hip. "You may be able to out-eat me, but I can certainly drink you under the table," he informed her, looking down at her face illuminated by the flickering lights on the buildings. She was stubborn, willful, endearing, warm, passionate, crazy and, most important, all his.

No, not *all* his, Greg silently amended. For a while she would be his, and if he worked it right, she just might be around when Hairy Harry lost his popularity and Tilly Cook would have to come up with a new idea. He knew if he was smart he'd work on cementing their relationship as soon as possible.

Mahoney's was crowded and smoke-filled as usual. Tank lifted a beefy arm in greeting and waved them in the direction of a rear table.

"Hi, want your usual?" Cari, one of the regular waitresses, asked.

"I think I'd like an Irish coffee instead," Jill decided.

"Same here," Greg agreed, slanting a wide grin in Jill's direction.

Two minutes later Tank stood in front of their table, his tattooed arms crossed in front of his brawny chest.

"What the hell is going on that you have to order a broad's drink?" he demanded of Greg. "A bourbon drinker doesn't order something that has whipped cream on it." He scowled at Jill as if it were all her fault.

"Tank, you deserve the top MCP award of the year." Jill took her cigarette and lighter out of her purse. "Tank doesn't mind if I smoke, do you?" She looked up at the hulk of a man who was never seen without a cigar jutting out of the corner of his mouth.

"Hey, sweetheart, they're your lungs," he grunted, moving away. "Your drinks will be on the way."

True to his word, Jill's Irish coffee arrived, but Greg received a bourbon and water.

"The man never listens," Greg grumbled, amid Jill's soft laughter.

Once when Greg excused himself and another man approached Jill asking her to dance, Tank showed up gruffly ordering the man to shove off.

"When're you going to put the poor slob out of his misery?" Tank asked as he pulled up a chair, spun it around and straddled the seat, his arms resting along the back.

"I didn't realize I was acting so mean to Greg." She had no trouble knowing who he was talking about.

"Come on, Jill, I'm not some idiot who just fell off the turnip truck," he retorted. "Anybody with halfassed sense can see how you two feel for each other."

Jill's rose-tinted fingernails slowly circled the rim of her mug as she looked down into the rich brown contents with the fancy mound of whipped cream dotting the top. "We're not looking for declarations of undying love from each other." The statement sent a spasm through her vitals in punishment. But

170

wasn't that exactly what they wanted—no commitments?

"Just some healthy sex, huh?" he said bluntly.

"Stow it, Tank," Jill advised a bit too kindly, although her eyes betrayed a dangerous glitter. "You're treading on unsafe ground. There could even be land mines ahead."

The older man smiled, reaching out to pat her shoulder. "Thanks, I just got my answer." He stood up and replaced the chair in its rightful place. "I'll send you two another drink."

"You trying to out-drink me after all?" Greg asked as he slid into his chair.

Jill shook her head. She dragged on her cigarette and stubbed it out in the ashtray.

Greg watched her every movement as if afraid she might disappear before his eyes. What was going through her head right now? She acted agitated, and he guessed Tank was the cause but he knew he wouldn't get an explanation out of either one of them.

"Let's go home," he entreated huskily, grabbing hold of her hand. "I'm tired of sharing you with other people."

Home. It was amazing how one word could sound so good to her. She wondered if it shouldn't have a deeper meaning than just a house they shared.

"Do you know something?" she murmured, tracing a pattern on the inner skin of his wrist with her fingernail. She raised shining eyes that were filled with promise. At that moment the raucous talk and music echoing through the room dissolved around them until they were the only two people left in the world. "I have this black lace nightgown I'd like to wear for you. Of course, there's not a lot of lace, or much of anything else, but . . ."

Greg tugged on her hand and pulled her out of her chair and out of the bar.

Jill never had a chance to show off her nightgown that night, much less wear it.

CHAPTER TEN

Two days later Jill rummaged through her apartment, and when she came up emptyhanded, she headed downstairs to search her office.

"Lose your favorite paper clip?" Greg inquired, sauntering into her office.

"No." Jill pulled open a drawer and flung papers over her shoulder until she reached the bottom.

He shrugged as if her erratic behavior was nothing unusual at ten o'clock in the morning.

"I'm going down to the store for some coffee and bread. Do you need anything?" he asked, interested in the way her rust wool sweater pulled away from the waistband of her jeans and revealed a creamy expanse of bare skin. His fingers itched to trace that same area, as he had done so many nights.

Jill's head snapped up. "Greg, you're a lifesaver," she said, now opening another drawer and pulling out some money. "Would you pick up a carton of cigarettes for me? I'm completely out."

Greg made a sound of disgust. "You can't even last out the morning, can you? Next thing you know you'll be suffering from a nicotine fit. I'd sure love to see a color picture of your lungs."

Jill's eyes narrowed, her shoulders thrust back and her stance wide in preparation for battle. "You make it sound as if I was some kind of addict." She spoke softly, her hands resting lightly on her hips. "I'll have you know that if I wanted to quit smoking, I could do it just like that." She snapped her fingers.

"Then do it," he dared.

"I have no reason to want to quit," she hedged. "My doctor said I'm very healthy, and I'm certainly not a heavy smoker."

Greg stepped forward, nudging Jill until she was backed against the wall, imprisoned by an arm on either side of her shoulders.

"Coward," he jeered softly, inclining his face into hers.

Jill blinked, afraid her eyes would cross if Greg's face drew any closer. "I'm not a coward. I couldn't dance as much as I do if I didn't have healthy lungs and no respiratory problems. There's no reason for me to quit, but if there were, I could easily give it up."

"Prove it." His breath warmed her lips.

Jill raised her chin a fraction of an inch. "Why should I?" she challenged.

A slow smile broke across Greg's lips. One hand moved until his thumbs grazed her soft, wool-covered shoulder. "We could always bet on it."

"Bet what?" She looked suspicious that he was so amiable all of a sudden.

"Dinner." Jill relaxed. That didn't sound so bad. "If you quit smoking for six months, I'll take you out to dinner to any restaurant of your choice. If you sneak a cigarette during that time, you'll take me," Greg explained.

"Piece of cake." She couldn't feel more confident about it.

"And the winner chooses where we eat," he reminded her.

"Fine by me."

"Good, because I choose Paris," he announced, looking much too smug.

"Paris!" Jill shrieked, pushing Greg away. "And I suppose I'm expected to pay the air fare also?"

"I was willing to pay cab fare for you," he retorted innocently.

Jill stalked across the room, hesitated, turned on her heel and faced Greg with her temper threatening to erupt like an angry volcano at any moment.

"You really don't think I can do it, do you?"

"I think you can do anything you set your mind to. The trouble is, you're easily bored the moment the challenge is gone," he replied. "This is something you're going to have to stick to no matter what."

"Meaning you honestly don't believe I can quit smoking for six months. I guess I'll just have to prove you wrong, won't I?" She tossed her head, looking up with a haughty smile on her lips. "I accept your bet." She stuck out her hand. "Shall we shake on it, or do you want my promise in writing so you can have it notarized?"

Greg chuckled, moving forward until he stood in front of her. "Oh, no, babe, I have my own method of sealing our bargain," he murmured, pulling her into his arms and settling his mouth on hers. For long moments his lips angled over hers in tantalizing caresses until a soft whimper sounded deep in Jill's throat. Greg lifted his head until their lips barely touched. *"That's* the way to seal a bargain."

"Mmm." Jill's fingers dug into his scalp, drawing him back for more. "I think we should discuss the terms further."

By evening Jill was still convinced that going without a cigarette would be easy. After dinner they played Trivial Pursuit, which Greg won, and they

175

retired to bed after a leisurely shower. The more confident Jill felt about the bet, the more fun she had debating exotic dinner destinations.

"Hong Kong would be nice," she mused, lying in the warm circle of Greg's arms after their lovemaking.

"For what?" he asked sleepily, shifting his weight until he lay on his side.

"For my dinner, of course."

"Don't be so sure of yourself. You've got roughly one hundred and seventy-nine more days to go," Greg reminded her. "Look how upset you were just this morning when you realized you had run out of cigarettes."

"I'll do it; you'll see. Let me see—Vienna has great food. So does Madrid. I've always been curious to see Lisbon."

Greg sighed. All he wanted to do was sleep, and Jill was already planning her success. It wasn't that he thought she was weak; she was stronger than many men he knew. No, it was just that smoking was one of her pleasures and she wasn't a woman to give up her pleasures easily. He was just glad they weren't giving up sex!

"Go to sleep," he ordered, stifling a yawn. "You've got plenty of time to plan your victory. And believe me, I'd like nothing more than to take you to Moscow for dinner if that's where you want to go."

The following day Jill suffered a few urges for a cigarette, but nothing she couldn't stop by nibbling on a candy bar. She knew she'd have to stop her pacifier method soon, before the extra calories caught up with her. In self-defense she signed up for an additional dance class.

By the end of one week Jill was well on her way to feeling like a raving maniac.

"Can't we ever get any sun around here?" she grumbled, staring out her office window at the heavy fog that covered the glass like a wool blanket. "This is the Sunshine State, or did the weather bureau miss that particular piece of information?"

"What happened to your love for all our spooky fog?" Greg questioned, perching his hip on a corner of her desk.

"Who could love anything so vile?" Jill scoffed, digging into a bright yellow ceramic bowl filled with shelled sunflower seeds and popping several into her mouth. "Fog is for Sherlock Holmes and Sam Spade."

"Yes, it does fit the image, doesn't it?" Greg agreed mildly.

Jill silently decided that his easygoing, get-along-with-Jill manner was definitely getting on her nerves. Every time she tried to pick an argument with him, he merely smiled and allowed her taunts to roll off his back as easily as water flowed off a duck. A bit of primal scream therapy would come in handy about now, she decided silently.

"You know, Greg, there have been days when I haven't liked you very much," she told him in a semi-sweet, honeyed tone. "But that's nothing compared to what I'm feeling toward you right now."

Greg nodded, as if he had expected her confession. "It's just nicotine withdrawal," he assured her. "Honey, you get this way once a month anyway, so it's nothing new to me."

"Once a month?" Jill shrieked, throwing her hands up in horror. She advanced on him with murder in her eyes. "Why, you—you chauvinist of the first degree. Just because you were born a male, you figure the slightest change in a woman's emotions is due to a biological function. People like you are the reason the pill was invented!" Her voice rose shrilly with each word.

Greg winced. He wondered how long Jill's tantrums were going to last, because he found that his patience was running dangerously low with each passing day. "You're hitting below the belt with that one, sweetheart," he warned softly.

"You got it, buster!"

"Look, I understand that you're feeling a bit irritable . . ." A bit? Last night they had gone out for Chinese food and it wasn't until they ordered that Jill announced she would have preferred Mexican. "But soon this testy mood will be all over and you'll be back to your old lovable self again," he concluded cheerfully. Please, be back to your old lovable self very soon! he thought desperately.

Jill's smile put Greg on the defensive. "Perhaps I'm better off this way. Who knows, you just might beg me to call off the bet."

Greg shook his head, guessing her devious intent. "No way, lady. I intend to support you in this all the way."

"Don't be so nice to me, Greg," she advised, her eyes glittering with their own battle signs. "In fact, you've been so sweet and amiable that I'm getting cavities just being around you. Now if you'll excuse me, I have a lunch date with Janine." She stalked off to her apartment.

Greg hid his smile until Jill was out of sight. She was magnificent when she was incensed. With each passing day she proved to be less tractable, but he was determined to see this through with her. He had a strong feeling that the next six months were going to seem more like six years.

Jill changed into an ecru silk shirt and soft green plaid skirt that just brushed the top of her taupe leather high-heeled boots. She draped two of her favorite gold chains around the blouse neckline and topped it with a blazer that matched her skirt. She had allowed her hair to curl riotously with only a comb along each side for control. She glanced at her bedroom clock and knew she'd have to hurry not to be late. She used a glossy pink lipstick and left the house.

"I'm surprised you're not having me swear a blood oath before I leave the house," she said waspishly when Greg followed her downstairs to the garage.

"I thought about it, but I figured I could trust you." He smiled, leaning against the passenger door of his car.

The expression in Jill's eyes told him her opinion of his reply. "Keep it up and I'll invite my mother for a long visit," she threatened.

Greg shuddered at the thought, but knew she would never carry it out. "You'd never do that to me. You can't get along with her after two minutes in her company."

"Don't bet on it," she replied succinctly, activating the electric garage door opener and opening her car door. She backed out and swung onto the street with her last view of Greg waving and telling her to have a good time.

By the time Jill met Janine at a café not far from the financial district, her mood had lightened considerably.

"I like your outfit," Janine greeted her, resembling an exotic bird in a peacock and fuchsia plaid skirt and a peacock silk blouse. A shawl matching her skirt was slung rakishly over one shoulder. "How is it going?"

Jill's smile felt very tight on her face. "Just fine."

"Good afternoon. Would you care for smoking or nonsmoking?" the hostess asked.

"Non," Janine said swiftly, seeing the look of desperation on Jill's face.

Since the morning fog had lifted, they were led outside to a patio area and seated amid leafy green plants. The two women accepted the menus and opened them to peruse the contents.

"The spinach quiche sounds good," Janine commented, looking up.

Jill stared at the menu as if the words meant her life or death. Holding the large dark blue pasteboard up slightly, she carefully scanned the other diners seated nearby. Her stealth would have been applauded by a private detective as she checked out each occupied chair. She inched up until only her eyes were seen above the menu.

"Janine," she whispered.

Janine looked up, surprised at the urgency coloring Jill's voice.

"Do you have any cigarettes on you?" Jill asked, keeping her voice low, as if afraid of being overheard.

"Jill, you know I don't smoke," Janine replied.

"But you could go out to the lounge and buy a pack," Jill insisted.

"No, I couldn't."

"Yes, you could," Jill hissed, laying her menu down and placing her hands on top of it.

"Oh, Jill." Janine's smile was as benign as the one Greg had been giving her the past few days. "You know you can't do that," she spoke to Jill the way she would talk to a small child. "After all, you and Greg made a bet, and you don't want to lose it, do you? That's why we all want to help you."

Jill sighed as the significance of Janine's words sunk in. "Just who all knows about this bet of the century?"

"Everyone listed in your address book."

Jill groaned. *"Everyone?"*

Janine nodded. "From Karen Adams to Jeannie Zach. You don't have a chance in trying to cheat. Deep down you don't really want to anyway."

Jill groaned again.

"Jill." Janine's voice portrayed disapproval. "You wouldn't really try to cheat, would you?"

She sighed, knowing very well she couldn't because to do so meant betraying Greg's trust and she could never hurt him in that way. She smiled and shook her head. "No, I'd never do it," she murmured, then quickly brightened. "How's your love life?" The look on Janine's face gave Jill her answer. "Aha! Obviously the two of you are getting along *very* well," she teased, enjoying making her friend blush. "Have you set the date yet?"

"Give us some time," she begged. "Besides, you and Greg will probably tie the knot before we do."

"What gives you that idea?" Jill asked carelessly, although she experienced a twisting sensation in the pit of her stomach at the idea of marrying Greg. It wasn't an unpleasant idea; in fact, it sounded very good. That was the problem, since Greg could very well have been the man who invented the word *bachelor*.

"Jill, do you know what you want to eat?" Janine broke into her thoughts.

"Huh?" Her head shot up. "Oh, I'll have the chicken and mushroom crepes, a small salad with your parmesan dressing and white wine," she mumbled, handing the menu to the waiter.

"I'll have the same," Janine decided. "Now, what about Greg?"

"He's fine," Jill evaded. "In fact, the new outline will be finished this week."

Janine shook her head. "Come on, Jill, when are you going to own up that you love him?"

Jill almost dropped the water glass she had picked up. "You make it sound like a disease," she retorted.

"For two people who reportedly enjoy their freedom, you both now spend all your time together instead of the eighty percent you used to. You might as well get married. Look at it as a tax deduction," Janine quipped.

"I won't be just a tax break for anyone," Jill muttered. From there her mood went rapidly downhill. After eating and listening to Janine advise her to indulge in some heavy thinking, Jill went shopping. But even that forced her to think about Greg and the time they had been interviewed for a writers' magazine. When asked if they had any hobbies, Greg had cheerfully informed the woman that Jill's hobby was buying clothes.

By the time she returned home she had enough packages to fill the backseat of her car.

"Ah, we've cleaned out the stores again, have we?" Greg eyed the many bags in Jill's arms when she passed his office.

"Yes, and there're more in the car," she informed him.

He took the hint. "Right away, milady."

Jill was busy hanging up her purchases when Greg entered her bedroom with the rest of the bags.

"I think you'll need another closet." He dropped the packages on the bed.

"Not all of it is for me," Jill announced smugly, searching through the bags until she found the one she wanted. She drew out a bright red and white box with a white ribbon tied in a saucy bow on top. She suddenly felt very shy, although this wasn't the first time she had brought him a surprise. "This is for you." She refused to look at his face.

Greg glanced down at the box thrust into his hands. He carefully loosened the bow and dropped the ribbon to the carpet. The top went next, and he loosened the gold sticker holding the white tissue paper together. Inside was a pearl gray sweater flecked with blue. The wool was so soft it reminded him of the texture of Jill's hair.

"Honey, it's beautiful." He found it difficult to get the words past his clogged throat. "It has the color of both our eyes."

She braved a glance at him. "You like it?"

He suddenly grinned. "It sure beats that Santa Claus bikini underwear you got me once. In fact, I love it." He pulled her into his arms for an energetic hug.

"Greg, you're squashing your sweater," Jill protested, but she couldn't resist returning the hug.

"Why don't you model your new clothes for me?" he whispered in her ear.

Jill got as far as trying on a pair of shoes before Greg stripped her clothing off and made love to her amid the paper bags and shoe boxes.

When he eased between her legs, she looked up at the rapture written on his face, aware the same could be seen on her features. Jill knew no one else would ever give her such joy, and the thought of losing Greg as her lover and friend saddened her.

After all, could their friendship still survive when the affair was over? But she didn't want to end their affair . . . not when she loved him so much.

Jill turned over and stared at the winking red light of the digital clock; three A.M. She half-turned to see that Greg was still asleep. She smiled at the man sprawled on his stomach, one arm curved around the pillow and a lock of hair lying across his forehead. At times like this Jill wanted to snuggle up to Greg and just hibernate for five or ten years. She might have awakened him and performed the great seduction scene of the century but for one minor problem—Jill wanted a cigarette so badly she was ready to kill for one. She glanced at the clock. Three-o-one.

Jill flopped onto her back and stared up at the pseudofootprint on the ceiling. When she had told Greg about it, he looked up and laughed, agreeing it did indeed resemble a footprint, but while he was athletic, he wasn't *that* good.

Three-o-two. Jill felt as if her insides were one giant rubber band, stretching tighter with every passing second. At three-o-three she was past coherent thought as she threw the covers from her, shivering when the frigid air washed over her bare skin. Jill grabbed Greg's green wool sweater that lay on the carpet and pulled it over her head. She glanced back to make sure that he was still asleep, and crept quietly out of the room.

Jill made her way downstairs easily thanks to a night light burning at the foot of the stairs. When she reached her office, she switched on the desk lamp and proceeded to carefully search every drawer in the large room. She finished with the desk and moved on to the credenza, squatting and balancing herself on her heels as she explored the deep interior.

"It's clean as a whistle."

Jill shrieked, losing her balance and falling smack on her bottom.

"You could have given me a heart attack, sneaking up on me like that!" she accused.

The cold air didn't seem to affect Greg, who wore only a pair of jeans with the snap undone and the zipper hovering at the top. His arms were crossed in front of his chest, and the expression on his face tore right through her. Greg didn't appear too angry, merely disappointed, and the sorrow in his eyes hurt her more than any show of temper.

"I, ah, I was looking for the pages we worked on today," she managed lamely.

He shook his head, looking very weary. "We both know better, Jill. Why don't you come up to bed?"

"Stop acting so nice to me!" she shouted, pounding the carpet with her fists. "I hate you when you sound like Mr. Rogers! And don't you dare smile and tell me this is just some kind of phase!" she ordered, shaking a fist at him.

Greg walked slowly toward her, looking like a lion stalking his prey. When he reached her he leaned down, grasped her by the elbows and pulled her up to her knees.

"You're just going through a bad time," he explained calmly, squatting on his heels in front of her. "You should have woken me up and we could have talked."

"I don't want to talk," she argued stubbornly. "I want a cigarette."

"Well, you can't have one!" he yelled back, now having lost all patience with her. "You promised to quit for six months, and by God, you're going to do it if it kills you!"

"Oh, sure, you'd like that, wouldn't you?" Jill blazed. "I'm to the point where I'm dying for a cigarette, except that you don't care. You don't understand how hard this is for me, so how can you claim to help me?"

"I most certainly do know all about it," Greg rapped out, straightening before reaching down to pull her to her feet. "I began smoking when I was fifteen because all my friends did. Three years later I was smoking four packs a day. When I was twenty-one I decided smoking and jogging didn't mix, so I gave up smoking. I was a regular bastard for months. There are times I still crave a cigarette."

Jill's mouth dropped open at Greg's revelation. "You never told me."

"You should have been able to guess." He grinned wryly, wrapping his hand around the back of his neck. "Ex-smokers are the worst enemies to smokers."

"Then you should have been more sympathetic toward me." Jill's temper was rising again.

"Jill, you're the damnedest little shrew I know." Greg blew up. "Why I want to marry such a temperamental woman I'll never know."

"I wouldn't—" The meaning of his words sank in suddenly. Jill snapped her mouth shut, then tentatively asked, "You want to marry me?" She felt as if she had been hit with a ten-ton weight.

"Why should I, when all you do is bitch every time I try to help you?" he railed at her, pacing back and forth. "And what do I get for my pains? You either yell at me or argue with me. I don't have to take this from anyone, so why should I take it from you?" He turned on her, his anger still on a roll.

186

"Greg, why do you want to marry me?" Jill asked softly, putting out a hand to halt his frenzied pacing.

"Why? That really takes the cake, Jill," he taunted. "Probably because I'm a masochist and I enjoy the way you drive me crazy twenty-four hours a day. Or maybe because I haven't met anyone as sweet and loving as you, when you're so inclined, and there's no one else I would prefer spending the rest of my life with. The best reason I know of is that I love you!" he yelled at the top of his lungs.

"I love you too!" Jill shouted back, then stifled a giggle. "Why are we yelling at each other?"

Greg shook his head. "Probably because it's what we do best."

She arched an inquisitive eyebrow. "If that's what we do best we're in big trouble."

Greg stopped and picked her up in his arms. "Well, then, why don't we see who's right?" he murmured, rubbing his nose against hers. "It's cold. At least you're healthy." He carried her into the conference room and set her on the small oval table.

"Greg, what are you doing?" She flinched when her bare bottom made contact with the cold wood.

"I'm fulfilling one of my fantasies," he explained, unzipping his jeans and pushing them down. "For months I've dreamed of making love to you on this table. Now I intend to do just that."

Jill laughed shakily. "Isn't it a bit cold down here?" She could see the goose bumps mapping her thighs.

"I'll warm you soon enough." Greg moved between her legs, making sure she felt his potent arousal throbbing against her thigh. His tongue drew a line over her cheekbone and down to her lips. "You always taste so good," he murmured.

Jill could feel herself sinking fast. "It must be my strawberry cleanser," she breathed, darting her tongue out to meet his.

"I always did like strawberry." His tongue rubbed against hers and allowed her to draw him into the warm cavern of her mouth. "Especially on you."

As their tongues met again, Greg's hands fastened on Jill's hips under the large sweater, kneading the satiny texture of her skin. With his fingers splayed out, his thumbs just brushed against the aching juncture of her thighs, never once touching the moist area in between.

Jill clasped her hands to the sides of Greg's head, her rose-tipped fingers digging into the soft dark hair. Soft whispers traveled up her throat to be captured by Greg's mouth. One of his hands slid over her stomach and moved up to caress the top of her breast with the back of his knuckles.

"Touch me, Greg," she pleaded in the throaty voice he only heard during their lovemaking. "Touch me."

"I could use some tactile stimulation myself," he panted, grabbing hold of her earlobe with his teeth and tugging gently.

Jill reached down to caress his hot, velvety skin, feeling his pulsing power. She touched him in ways that she knew drove him crazy and smiled at the raw words he whispered in her ear.

In one abrupt movement Greg had the sweater drawn up to Jill's neck and over her head. He enclosed a nipple in his mouth, pulling on it until the electric currents made their way down to the center of Jill's femininity. She cried out, moving her hips against him and winding her legs around his waist. She dipped her own head to find the tiny brown nipple hidden among the dark crisp hair and bring it to life under her loving mouth. She worried it with teeth and tongue until it rose up as hard as her own and brought that same erotic ache to Greg.

"Take me into you, Jill," he ordered hoarsely. "Show me you want me as much as I want you."

She circled him with her fingertips and led him on a journey into a hot sensual world. What she began, he finished. Once she had guided him, he thrust deeply into her once, twice, until she was filled with his power. Jill held on tightly as Greg delved even deeper into her femininity. Their mouths mated as frantically as their bodies did, love tempering the raw hunger that urged them on.

Jill knew she was reaching for the ultimate and that Greg was beside her. When the moment came they cried out together and remained still, holding each other as the small aftershocks settled within them.

Jill nestled her face against Greg's shoulder, licking the salt from his damp skin.

"Did you mean it when you said you loved me?" he murmured, rubbing his hands up and down her back.

"Yes." She kissed his shoulder. "We'll always argue, you know."

"But think of all the wonderful making up we'll do." He rested his cheek against her hair. "As much as I'd like to stay here, my buns are freezing." He gathered Jill up in his arms and carried her upstairs to their warm bed. Once they were settled among the covers, they began making plans for the future.

"We could knock out the dividing wall and convert this into one large apartment," Jill suggested, yawning deeply. The intensity of their loving and her sleepless night had finally caught up with her.

"I had wanted to take you out to a romantic restaurant and give you the proper atmosphere for my marriage proposal," Greg said apologetically, with a contrite expression on his face. "I'm sorry for yelling it at you."

"You certainly made up for it later," she countered, running her hand over the breadth of his chest and down to his flat stomach as she rested her head on his shoulder. She took a deep breath before admitting, "I lost the bet, Greg, as surely as if I had lit up."

"You weren't smoking," he corrected.

"No, but if I had found a cigarette, I would have smoked it right away." She sighed. "Therefore I owe you dinner in Paris." She reached across his chest for the phone.

"What are you doing?" Greg asked, watching her place the phone on his quilt-covered stomach and dial.

Jill held up her hand, indicating silence. "Hello? Yes, I'd like to make two reservations, first-class." She smiled at Greg. "To Paris. Does that flight lay over in Dallas or Houston? Hello?" She looked down at Greg's fingers pressing down on the disconnect button.

"Dallas and Houston are in Texas," he informed her.

"So is Paris." She dropped a kiss on his nose, sliding down to his mouth. "You never specified *which* Paris. Besides," she murmured against his mouth, "everyone dreams of going to Paris, France, for a special dinner. How many think of somewhere quiet and out of the way like Paris, Texas?"

190

"I knew there was a reason I wanted to marry you," he replied.

"Prove it."

He did.

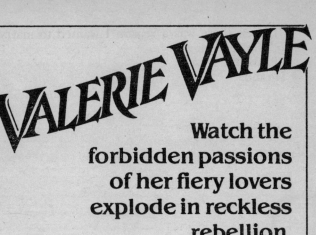